A MURDER
OF
CROWS

Also by Partick Buchanan

A Parliament of Owls

A MURDER
OF
CROWS

PATRICK BUCHANAN

𝔰𝔡

STEIN AND DAY/Publishers/New York

FIRST STEIN AND DAY PAPERBACK EDITION 1985

A Murder of Crows was originally published in hardcover by Stein and Day/*Publishers* in 1970.

Stein and Day/*Publishers*
Scarborough House
Briarcliff Manor, N.Y. 10510

ISBN 0-8128-8179-6

For Ed Corley and Jack Murphy
without whom this book could
not have been written.

A MURDER OF CROWS

1

A few minutes before three in the afternoon the crow exploded. The Kentucky road was full of chuckholes, and I had slowed down to save the Cadillac Fleetwood's springs. I was so intent on my driving that I didn't see the crow depart this life.

But Charity Tucker did. She sucked in her breath and her hand grabbed my leg.

"Ben, stop!"

I hit the brakes. The Fleetwood skidded on the gravel and, for a frightening second, skittered toward the shoulder.

"What is it, baby?"

"Back up. To that stump."

I put the car in reverse and inched back toward a large stump hulking just off the shoulder.

Charity laughed nervously. "I saw it explode," she said.

"Saw what explode?"

She pointed at the stump. "A crow. A big black crow. He was perched on that stump. And he exploded."

"Sure," I said. "One of those kamikaze crows. They're always sending them out on suicide missions."

She went over to the stump. Beyond it a drop-off slanted down to a patch of blackberry bushes.

"I saw him," she repeated.

"You're a poor bewildered city girl," I said. "You're not used to being out here in the boondocks. You have what we ridge runners call mountain fever. The first symptom is hallucinating things like exploding crows."

She bent over and picked up a feather. It was jet black. She held it out to me.

"Explain this, Ben." I took the feather. One end was soaked in bright red blood.

"All right," I said. "So a crow exploded. Happens every day."

A raucous caw sounded from a tree above us. We looked up. A very angry bird perched on a branch was conveying, crow-style, how unimpressed he was by our ancestry, our appearance, and our presence. In no uncertain terms he invited us to be on our way.

"There's your exploding crow," I said. "He's just been in a fight and lost a couple of feathers."

"I know what I saw," Charity said stubbornly.

I took her arm and started to lead her back to the car. Behind us there came a sound like a wet paper bag being burst. I turned just in time to see what was left of our crow friend tumbling down toward the blackberry patch.

Charity gave me a look of triumph. "There," she said. "What did I tell you?"

"In the car," I said. "Fast."

"Why?"

"Because some bastard's shooting at us, that's why." I shoved her inside and ran around the front of the Fleetwood to get in from the driver's side.

"I didn't hear any shots."

I ground the starter. "He might be two hills away. The valleys are swallowing up the sound."

The car moved forward, then lurched as we heard the sharp explosion.

"He got our right front tire," Charity said calmly.

I put the Fleetwood in low and started forward. A second explosion announced the demise of the right rear tire. The car now leaned to the right like an unbalanced seesaw. I kept grinding up the hill, wincing at the thought of rims cutting through my fifty-dollar white sidewalls.

We had made less than ten feet when there was a new sound: a hammer striking an anvil? The whole car quivered under the impact. A spray of steam and water burst from its hood.

11

I turned off the key before the engine could tear itself to pieces.

"He put one through the radiator," I said unnecessarily. Charity sat stiffly beside me, her lips drawn tight.

"What now?"

I opened my door and got out. My muscles were tight, awaiting the shattering impact of the bullet that might come at any second. I gave it a full minute. Nothing happened.

"Crawl out," I told Charity. "On this side."

She slid under the wheel and stood beside me. I closed the door and took her arm.

"Now we walk," I said. "Slowly. Don't look back. Just keep your eyes on the road."

We had taken perhaps four steps when the gravel in front of us erupted in a puff of dust. The bullet whined as it ricocheted into the trees.

Charity let out a little cry and started to pull away from me. I held her arm hard and drew her back.

"Don't run!" I said. "He isn't trying to hit us. But you might throw off his aim."

Another shot, closer this time. Charity winced, and her left hand began to bleed where a sliver of rock had struck the knuckle.

"Just another hundred feet," I said, talking in a soft voice as we walked along that nakedly exposed road, the hot Kentucky sun beating down on our unprotected heads.

Charity did not answer. Another bullet peppered us with gravel. She did not break her stride or make a sound.

The last fifty feet to the crest of the hill seemed like a mile. The unseen rifleman did not fire again. As we got closer to safety, the urge to run became almost unbearable.

I kept talking to Charity. She still had not made a sound. But tears had cut wet paths through the gray dust that had settled on her face.

"We're almost there, baby," I said. "Whoever he is, he's a crack marksman. Probably thought we were revenuers and decided to give us a scare."

My girl didn't answer. I didn't expect her to. Once, she stumbled and almost fell.

We reached the crest of the hill. This was the part I feared. Our rifle-toting friend on the mountain could very well have been playing with us, letting us get almost to safety before exploding our heads the way he had the two crows.

But we passed over the top and into the shelter of the sunlit valley beyond. Half a mile ahead I could see a crossroad, and to the right a gas station.

"Oh, *Ben!*" Charity sagged against me. I helped her to the rotting trunk of a fallen elm tree and sat beside her, holding her close as the terror came out of her in noisy sobs.

2

I had a hard time convincing myself that I was really on the road to Gethsemane, Kentucky. You have to have good eyesight to find Gethsemane on any map. It is a tiny place that nestles in the foothills of the Appalachian Mountains. It had taken me a day and a half of hard driving to get down from New York, and I hadn't wanted to come in the first place. I wanted to stay on my out-of-the-way lake in upstate New York, drink beer, and stalk the elusive trout.

You've already met Charity Tucker. She is tall and blonde and very beautiful. She is also very stubborn.

"Ben," she had insisted back in New York, "Subrinea Brown's one of my oldest friends. We were in college together. When she sounds as terrified as she did on that phone, there's something more serious involved than our finding out why her father's being harassed by a couple of crooked officials."

"Colonel Brown wants to open a racetrack," I said. "My bet is, the officials want a piece of the action."

"That wouldn't frighten Subrinea like this," Charity said. "Ben, we've got to help her."

Charity is the Tucker of "Shock and Tucker—Investigations." I am the Shock. Benjamin Lincoln Shock, ex-cop, unlicensed trouble-shooter, and known sucker for tall blondes who hang onto my arm and whisper, "Please, Ben."

So the next thing I knew, my black Fleetwood was bounding along a Kentucky back road, heading into blue grass country.

As the road curved through a valley, we passed a shapeless smear of fur and meat, crushed in the center of the highway. An odor, pungent and yet not unpleasant, swept through the car.

Charity wrinkled her nose.

I laughed. "Skunk."

"Ugh," she said.

A dog came out of the bushes and loped along beside the car, barking at the tires. He was a flop-eared, gawky-legged hound. When I hit the gas, he gave up and sat on the shoulder, howling in frustration.

"The Gethsemane Chamber of Commerce

16

welcoming committee," I said. "Gethsemane? Where do they get names like that?"

"You're in the middle of the Bible Belt," Charity said. "It's the only book a lot of these hill people own. In an odd way, they all try to live by the Word."

I didn't dispute her. I have learned not to disagree with Charity Tucker on matters of fact. She has more gray matter inside that lovely head than females are supposed to possess. Before I met her she was a top TV newsgirl, and when she says something, you can be positive she has checked it out nine ways from Sunday.

"There's a sign," she said.

I slowed. A rude wooden marker pointed into a gravel road that led away from the highway: "GETHSEMANE, 6 MI."

Dust boiled up behind us as we turned.

"What the hell is anyone doing with a race track six miles off the main highway?" I grumbled.

"Subrinea's father started out owning and training horses," Charity said. "He intends to combine that with running the track. Besides, people in these parts will drive fifty miles to see a horse race."

I looked at the steep hills, heavily wooded with oak and walnut trees. It had been ten minutes since we'd seen another car, and there wasn't a house in sight. The car wheels crunched on the gravel. Two crows flew across the road, cawing. A butterfly fluttered in through my window and perched on the dashboard.

"Scram," I said. "No hitchhikers."

We clattered across a wooden bridge. Far below it in a rocky gorge, water tumbled over mossy stones.

"Lovely," Charity said. I grunted, and she punched me in the leg. "You have no soul for beauty," she complained.

"Sure I do. I love to look at beautiful things. Like inch-thick steaks, with about a gallon of cold beer and a genuine Royal Jamaica corona. That's beauty."

She made an exasperated sound, but at last she smiled.

We came up a hill into the sunlight. The trees dappled the road with their swaying shadows.

That was when I slowed down for the chuckholes, and the first crow exploded.

Now we were on foot, with an unknown sniper somewhere behind us.

The half mile to the gas station was all downhill, but even so I was dripping sweat when we crunched into the empty drive. Charity had been silent during the long walk under the hot sun, although I had tried to cheer her up with some bad jokes about moonshiners and revenuers.

At first the station seemed deserted. Then a tall, slim young man wearing green work clothes came out of the garage. He blinked at us.

"Howdy. You folks have car trouble?"

"You could call it that," I said. "Got a tow car?"

He shook his head. "Nearest wrecker's down to Jim Hurley's in Gethsemane. I'd be pleased to call him for you, though."

"Thanks," I said. "We're about a half mile up the road, just over the crest of that hill."

"Hot day for walking."

Charity had been looking around. "Where's your ladies' room? she asked.

"Around there, near the car wash," said the attendant. "But I got to get the key for you. We keep it locked. Otherwise those field nigras slip in and use up all the soap."

Charity's lips tightened, but she waited patiently for the key, then disappeared around the corner of the building.

"Tire trouble?" the attendant asked.

"Two flats."

He whistled. I followed him inside. A pay telephone hung on the wall over the map rack.

"That's bad luck," he said.

"Tell your friend there's a hole in my radiator, too."

He whistled again. "What made that?"

"The same thing that made the holes in my tires. A high-powered rifle slug."

His hand, which had been reaching for the telephone, lowered slowly.

"How about it?" I said. "Are you going to call this friend with the tow truck?"

19

His eyes flickered nervously out the window. "I don't want no trouble with those hill people."

"What hill people?"

He made an exaggerated shrug.

"Listen," I said, "I'm running short on patience. Some character shot a lot of holes in my car. I had to walk down here under a hot sun. I am sweaty and thirsty, and all I want to do now is get my car hauled into town and vanish from your life forever. How about it?"

"Listen, mister," he said earnestly, "if the Unknown Tongue are shooting things up, they wouldn't take kindly to me prankin' with them. I'm surely sorry, but I got a wife and two young'uns. I don't hardly keep my nose above water as it is. If they was to sneak in here some night when I'm closed up, they could burn me right out of business."

"Sure," I said. "In that case, would you mind giving me change for a dollar? Maybe I can make the phone call myself."

He rang up No Sale on the register and gave me five dimes and two quarters in exchange for the dollar bill. "I surely am sorry," he said again, "but I just can't take no chances with the Unknown Tongue."

I sighed and bit. "What or who is the Unknown Tongue?"

He turned away and I knew he wasn't going to say anything more.

Charity came in. She had washed her face and

combed her hair and looked adorable again. She even managed a faint smile.

"Honey, how can we reach Subrinea?"

She spread her hands. "Her number's in my purse."

"And your purse is in the car."

She nodded. I sighed. "Okay, information it is." I put a dime in the slot, dialed 411, and asked the operator for the number of the Brown residence.

"Which Brown is that, sir?"

"Subrinea."

"Sorry, there is no listing for Subrinea Brown."

I muttered something, and she went on, "But you can reach her over at Mr. Loyal Boone's law office."

I started to ask her how she knew, but didn't. Small-town telephone operators could teach a few tricks to the CIA.

She gave me the number and I wrote it down on the corner of a Kentucky road map.

"Who's Loyal Boone?" I asked Charity.

"Subrinea's boy friend. He used to be the county attorney, but he resigned that job to handle the race track's legal business."

"Well, the operator says she's at his office. Here's the number. Why don't you give her a holler?"

Charity took the dime from the coin return, redeposited it, then dialed. When she got

Subrinea, she said, "We're out at the crossroads gas station on the gravel road. . . . No, I'll explain later. Can you pick us up?"

I touched her arm. "Tell her to have someone send out a tow truck."

During the phone conversation, the gas station attendant had slipped out of the office. I went out and looked along the road. he was nowhere in sight.

"Looks like our misfortunes shook him up," I said.

Charity stood up on tiptoe and kissed me. She smelled good. "Thanks, buster."

"Thanks for what?"

"Thanks for not saying anything about my womanly exhibition of the vapors."

"Forget it," I said. "I was feeling pretty vaporous myself."

We had a cigarette; then a dusty Ford appeared from the direction of town. A big, bluff man who looked like a thirty-year-old Victor McLaglen was driving. With him was a sandy-haired girl with round dark eyes that reminded me of a Keane painting.

We introduced around. He turned out to be Loyal Boone, and of course the blonde was Subrinea Brown. A big coffee-colored hound took up most of the back seat. "Meet Blue," said Loyal Boone.

"You girls wait here," I said. "Mr. Boone and I will drive up to the car and get the luggage out."

22

"We'll go with you," said Subrinea.

"It wasn't a suggestion," I told her. I opened the door and she got out. She was taller than Charity, with a ripe shape that stuck out in good places. I piled in and we headed up the gravel road in a cloud of dust. From the back seat Blue said, "Wurf."

"It might be smart to park this side of the hill crest," I told Loyal Boone. "There's somebody up in those mountains with a high-powered rifle, and he can part your hair with it."

"So I gathered." Instead of slowing up for the crest, he drove right up to the Fleetwood and stopped. I winced at the sight of the big car tilted insanely on both flat tires. Steaming water still dripped to the gravel under the shattered radiator.

"Whoever did it is gone," said Loyal, getting out. "These hill people have their own sense of humor. They didn't want to hurt you—just spook you a little."

Blue paid houndly honors to the undamaged left front tire while I unlocked the trunk and began unloading the suitcases. "I mentioned this to the gas station attendant and he practically dried up and blew away in front of me. He said something about Unknown Tongues."

"Could be," Loyal said. "We haven't had too much trouble with them lately, but all the fuss about Butterfield Downs is just the kind of thing that would stir them up again."

I got Charity's purse, then remembered my .38 Police Special in the glove compartment and took it out too.

Loyal nodded at it professionally. "Do you have a permit for that?"

"Not any more," I said. "I'll keep it in my suitcase."

"This is Kentucky," said Loyal. "The law on the books says you shouldn't have guns without a permit. But the law of the land says different."

"What's Butterfield Downs?" I asked.

"Colonel Brown's new track. His horse farm's called Butterfield Farm, so he used the same name."

"Isn't this kind of out of the way for a track?"

"Not too much," he said, starting the Ford. "This is just a small summer track. He plans to fit his meets in between those run at Keeneland and Miles Park. There's plenty of betting money to go around. But—and I mean no disrespect by this, Mr. Shock—you have to understand these hill people. Particularly the Unknown Tongue. Used to be, in this area, their religion was Baptist and Methodist. Why, we must have had about forty different kinds of Baptists alone—hardshell Baptists, free-will Baptists, forty-gallon Baptists. But when the preachers stopped talking about the utter sanctity of the Word and the churches gave up shouting and the old ways of getting saved, a lot of folks went over to the other sects."

"One of which, I gather, is Unknown Tongue."

"That's right. And they take a dim view of such heathen sports as horseracing."

"Is that why Miss Brown asked us down here?"

"Partly. Funny things have been happening. I suppose she told you about her father."

"She said he had a mild heart attack."

"That's true," said Loyal. "He's off the critical list, but they're keeping him in the hospital in Lexington for a week or so just to be safe." He took out a pack of Bull Durham and rolled a cigarette one-handed as we drove along the bumpy road. Then he pulled a kitchen match from a shirt pocket, struck it with his thumbnail, and lit up. He didn't notice me gawking. "What she doesn't know, because Adger Brown is a tough old buzzard and didn't want to worry her, is *why* he had that seizure."

"I gather he told you."

He nodded. "Adger came home from a little poker session at the Mayor's house and crawled into bed. He felt something cold wrap around his ankle and went about ten feet straight up in the air. Someone had slipped a five-foot copperhead under the sheets."

I shuddered. "Was he bitten?"

"No. He grabbed the copperhead by the tail and popped its head off, just like you snap a bullwhip. Then he belted down about five ounces of hundred-proof white lightning. The doctors swear that's what gave him the attack, and not the snake at all." Loyal laughed softly. It was obvious that he liked Adger Brown.

"Charity said she's never known Subrinea to sound as scared as she was when we talked to her. Why is that if she doesn't know about the attempt on her father's life?

"She's a sensitive girl, Mr. Shock."

"Make it Ben."

"Ben. It's not hard to see there's something dangerous going on. Adger Brown has lived in this county all his life. He plays poker with the Mayor and Senator Treffit. Our people look out for their own. Adger should have been given every break to help get Butterfield open. Instead, he's running into a stone wall. Permits are delayed. Inspectors condemn everything in sight."

"Maybe there's coal on the property," I suggested.

His laugh was bitter. "Thirty years ago I'd have said the same thing. But today the surest way to go broke is to discover coal on your land. It just isn't worth taking out of the ground any more." He threw the butt of his cigarette out the window. "No, there's something else. Maybe it's higher up than Buckhorn County. Maybe the state just doesn't want another track. It's hard to figure. Adger made careful inquiries before he committed himself to Butterfield. He didn't get any negative reactions last year. But now it's as if the well suddenly dried up."

We pulled into the gas station's driveway. The girls were inside drinking Dr. Peppers. Charity came out and handed one to each of us. I grinned at her, read the slogan, "Ten, Two, and Four," from the side, and slugged down half a bottle. The soda cut through the dust in my throat and caused a very ungentlemanly belch.

The girls climbed in the back seat over Blue's groaning protests. Loyal honked the horn, and after a minute honked it again.

The attendant came out of the back room, shading his eyes from the sun.

"Hey," he said. "Mister Boone. Howdy-do."

"Lommie Wingbright," said Loyal, "these people are friends of mine. Mighty good friends."

"Proud to meet them," said Lommie. He wiped his hand on his pants leg as if he were going to come over and offer it.

"They ever ask, you give them help," said Loyal.

"Why sure I will." Then he had to yell after us, because Loyal had floorboarded the Ford. "You-all come back, y'hear?"

"Lommie's a good enough man most times," said Loyal. "Trouble is, the good Lord forgot to equip him with a backbone."

"He really seemed to be scared of the Unknown Tongue," I said.

From the rear seat Subrinea Brown said, "I don't believe it was the Unknown Tongue."

"They're against your daddy's track, honey," said Loyal.

"They're against poker playing, too, but they haven't shot up Mayor Hornbuckle's Lincoln Continental. No, Mr. Shock, there's more going on in Gethsemane than a hill sect shouting down sinners. There's big money involved."

"Your daddy's put almost two million in Butterfield," said Loyal.

"And," she said grimly, "he's going to lose every dime of it if we don't find out who's behind all our troubles."

"What kind of troubles, other than inspectors condemning your wiring?" I asked.

"Butterfield's a small track," she said, "but Daddy wants it to be one of the best in the country. He's actually bought a lot of the equipment instead of leasing it, because we've got a year-round operation here with the farm and so we can provide maintenance. Most tracks can't afford to keep people on all year. But one piece of equipment we didn't want to buy is the Totalisator."

"What's a Totalisator?" asked stupid Ben.

"It's a computer and a bunch of wiring and lights that issues betting tickets and totes up the odds," said Charity sweetly.

"Oh." The only time I had ever been to the track was to stand watch on the pickpocket squad.

"It costs around two hundred thousand dollars a year to lease a Totalisator," said Subrinea, "but a track can't really operate without one. The old mechanical ways of figuring and displaying odds are just too slow for the modern horseplayer."

"What happened?"

"We had a series of accidents and thefts. We hired a photo-finish photographer, with his equipment, to shoot some practice races. The camera costs two thousand dollars, and the lenses run around six hundred dollars apiece."

"I get the picture," I said. "While the photographer was in the little boys' room, the camera walked."

"Right," said Subrinea. "It has to be harassment. A photo-finish camera has absolutely no value anywhere except at a race track. And no one would dare use that one at any other track in the world. The serial numbers were circulated within six hours after the theft."

"Tell him about the starting gate," said Loyal.

"You know what a starting gate is, don't you, Ben?" Charity asked. I gave her a dirty look. She blew me a kiss.

"It's basically a row of stalls on wheels with individual gates in front and back," said Subrinea. "The gates behind lock mechanically. The ones in front are under tension from heavy springs, held back by powerful electromagnets. When the starter pushes the button, the magnets let go and the springs slam the gates open all at once."

"Adger bought his own gate," said Loyal. "Most tracks lease them, but Adger figured he could use the gate for training horses as well as racing them."

"What does one of those gadgets cost?" I asked.

"In the neighborhood of thirty-five thousand dollars."

"Nice neighborhood."

"Someone got into the gate last week, Subrinea said, "and sprayed liquid solder over the magnet coils. Every one was shorted out. We had to disassemble them all and send for spares. Meanwhile, the gate is just a thirty-five-thousand-dollar hunk of metal."

"Does all this have anything to do with the Totalizer?" I asked.

"Totalisator," corrected Charity.

"Plenty," said Subrinea. "General Instrument doesn't sell Totalisators—they lease them. They provide the equipment and men to run it. But there's some question in their minds as to whether or not their equipment—or their personnel—would be safe at Butterfield. So we may have to go as far away as Australia to buy one."

"Which costs?"

"Somewhat over a million dollars."

I whistled. "I think I agree with you. This

doesn't sound like the work of one obscure religious sect."

"Don't underrate the Unknown Tongue, Ben," warned Loyal. "They exercise a lot of influence around here."

"Not as much," Subrinea said, "as whoever's trying to put my daddy out of business."

3

Seen down the last slope of the road, Gethsemane looked much like a hundred other small American towns I have driven through. We had left the gravel behind and were now on black asphalt. Occasional farms, set well back from the boundary fences, sprawled over the gentle hills on both sides of the road. Chickens scattered out of our way with frightened squawks at the horn of the Ford. Some were red, some were white, and some were speckled black. At one farm entrance five polka-dotted birds raced in front of the car, gobbling wildly.

"Guinea hens," said Loyal. "Best watchdogs in the world. Anyone comes within half a mile, they set up a ruckus that'd wake the dead. They're even louder than Blue here."

We passed a white church, its steeple leaning slightly to the south.

"Methodist," he said. "We've got two of those in town and five Baptist."

"Where do the Unknown Tongue hang out?"

"In the hills."

We came to a hanging spotlight and waited, although there was not another moving car in view, until it flashed green. Then we turned right, onto the main street.

It wasn't much. A Kroeger supermarket, a Woolworth five and ten, several smaller stores, and a Ritz theater with its front boarded up.

"Old Man Willoughby closed down the Ritz six years ago when the drive-in opened out on the Lexington Highway," said Loyal. "They were letting a whole carful of folks in for a dollar and he just couldn't meet the price. Besides, most houses have TV now, and people don't have that much cash money, to pay for what they get at home free."

We passed the courthouse, swung around the small square, and parked outside a low white office building. Gold lettering in the window read, "Loyal Boone, Attorney at Law."

The door was unlocked, and we went in. The main room was all rich wood and book-lined walls.

"I bought the books from Judge Jasper Holland," said Loyal. "For all I know, the pages may be blank."

Somehow I didn't believe him. This big, friendly Kentuckian radiated competence. He went back into the other office and returned with a sheaf of papers.

"Now," he said to Subrinea, "Where were we?"

"The option on the land for an extension of the parking area, and the backstretch section of cottages and workout track for boarded horses," she answered.

He riffled through the papers, giving Charity and me an apologetic look. "This'll just take a minute, and it's kind of important." He bit at his lip, studying the typewritten pages. Then he looked up. "It's all here, Subrinea. In fact, you've got about ten times as much land optioned as your daddy'll ever need."

"There's a reason for wanting the property all the way up over the top of Blood Mountain," she said. "Daddy's planning on developing that section one day, once the track's established. It'd have the best view in the valley."

"Well, the option's clean," said Loyal. "Of course you'll owe Mr. Mulhulland another payment September first."

"How much?"

"Eighty thousand dollars." He frowned. "That's pretty high for option money."

Subrinea laughed. "Some lawyer. The option cost us fifteen thousand. The eighty is earnest money. It'll be applied to the total price if we close before January first."

35

He squinted at the papers, nodded. "But if you don't close, you lose the eighty thousand plus the original fifteen."

It sounded like a lot of money. I could see now why the Browns needed help.

The door opened and a man swaggered in. He was about five feet tall and nearly as wide. He wore a carefully tailored slate-gray uniform shirt and pants with sewn-in creases. A huge badge was pinned to his left shirt pocket, and so help me God, it had a brass rifle cartridge mounted in its center.

"Howdy, Loyal," said the man. His huge paw rested lovingly on the ivory butt of his Colt .45, worn low and strapped down on his leg.

"Howdy," said Loyal without warmth. "Sheriff Matthew Goff, this is Miss Charity Tucker and Mr. Benjamin Shock from New York."

Goff nodded toward us curtly. "I heard about them. Loyal, now that you ain't county attorney no more, that puts you in the same boat with ordinary folks."

"What boat is that?"

"When there's a shooting, you are supposed to report it to the sheriff's office, fast as you can."

He actually said *ree-po't* and *sherf*.

"What shooting is that?"

Goff nodded at me. "These folks here."

"Hell," said Loyal, "it was just one of those hill boys getting off a little target practice. Nobody hurt, nobody got mad."

36

I noticed that when Loyal was talking to Goff the voice took on a pronounced Kentucky twang.

"That's up to me to decide, Loyal." Goff turned to me. "Now, Mister Shock, do you aim to make a complaint"

"Against whom?"

"Whoever took a shot at you."

"Not me," I said. "He's too good a shot. He might get mad and try to hit me next time."

"This ain't funny, mister," said Goff, bellying over to the chair I was sitting in. This made me nervous. Each of us has his own sense of space. You can sit across a table from me and we are each in our staked-out plot. Lean too far forward, push your way into the closeness that is part of my territory, and I become annoyed and uneasy. It's a law of life. Cops know this, and they use the territorial impulse to make suspects nervous.

I got up, smiled down at Mr. Five-by-Five, and put my hand on his shoulder. Now I was intruding into *his* territory. He didn't like it. He brushed away my hand.

"We're just visitors, Sheriff," I said. "We don't want to cause any trouble. Let's forget about the shooting. Like Mr. Boone said, someone probably had a little too much moonshine and started making like Sergeant York."

"I don't need any of your sass," he said. "What you're doin' here ain't no big secret. I didn't have to come over here to try to help out. But I don't want no smart Yankee lawyer comin' down here and sayin' you was conspired against. If you stick your hand in a copperhead's nest and get bit, that's your own doin', and Loyal Boone, you're my witness."

"I surely am," said Loyal. "You gave Mr. Shock a fair warning against copperheads."

"You know what I meant," Goff shot back. He headed for the door, turned for his exit line: "This is a clean town, even if it ain't New York City. Anybody who makes trouble answers to me."

He made his departure. Sheriff Goff had seen too many Western movies.

Loyal was frowning. "Who told him?"

"How about your friend, Brave Lommie?"

"Uh-uh. Lommie wouldn't call the Law if the Russians surrounded his station."

"Maybe the tow truck," I said.

"All I told them was that you had tire trouble. No," said Loyal, "it has to be whoever did the shooting."

"Maybe the guy wanted credit for his good marksmanship," I said.

"I know what you're getting at," said Subrinea. Loyal nodded. "The Unknown Tongue wouldn't call the Law. Subrinea, I'm beginning to think you're right. This thing goes deeper than the hill people."

Before anyone else could say something

bright, the telephone rang. Loyal picked it up, listened, said, "Just a minute," and handed the instrument to Subrinea. "It's Chuck Wallace out at the track," he said.

As she listened, her face went white. "We'll be right out."

She hung up, and Loyal stepped to her.

She shut her eyes and held out both hands. He took them.

"It's Jesse Simpson, she said. "He's dead."

His voice was harsh. "How?"

"Who's Jesse Simpson?" I asked.

"One of the gardeners at the track," said Loyal. He turned back to Subrinea. "What happened?"

"I don't know," she said. "All Chuck said was that Jesse just burned to death."

4

Some ten minutes out of town a wide, well-banked road turned off the blacktop, curving up a hill. White wooden fences lined both sides.

"We're trying to get blacktop put in here," Subrinea said glumly as Loyal's car hit gravel again. "But the permits haven't come through."

The fields were deep green, lined with rows of trees. In the distance, I saw several horses grazing in the shade.

"Chuck Wallace is Adger's trainer," Loyal said as we turned into a smaller drive off the main road. " He handled forty horses for Adger last year and won something over a million and a half in prize money."

I whistled. "So that's where Colonel Brown got the money for the track."

"Not on your life," said Loyal. "Adger made

his stake in tobacco. Any owner who more than breaks even these days is doing good. You can spend anywhere from five to twenty thousand dollars for a halfway decent horse, and another ten thousand a year for shipping, veterinary care, and hay. Plus your overhead and depreciation."

"That's quite a nut to get off," I said. "Now you'll tell me the average horse earns ten dollars a year."

Loyal laughed. "A little better than that, but not much. Put it around thirty-three hundred dollars. With a return like that, you've got to have a couple of real hot ones to stay out of the red."

"I suppose," I said, "that Kentucky ought to be thankful for tobacco."

We screeched up beside a long white barn. I still hadn't seen any sign of a racetrack.

"It's over the next hill," Loyal said in answer to my unspoken question. "Toward Blood Mountain."

Subrinea was still pale, but game. She said, "It used to be called Blue Ridge. There was an explosion in one of the mines and for two years the whole mountain was covered with smoke and dust. The flames inside the earth broke out and made the mountain look like it was covered with blood."

We found Chuck Wallace inside the barn. The

place smelled of horses and of hay. He was on the telephone, yelling at someone.

"How the hell do I know?" he bellowed. Chuck Wallace was a big, husky man with a totally bald head, and when he bellowed it filled the barn. I heard horses banging against their stalls.

"No, dammit!" Wallace roared. "I didn't see a goddamned thing. I heard him yell something awful, and when I ran back to the feed bin I found him lying on the floor. He was already dead, and his skin was smoking. . . . His *skin!* His clothes weren't even singed. . . . How the hell do I know why? Listen, Sheriff, Miss Brown's here now. I'll come in later and make a statement. Bye, now." He hung up and turned to us. "I sometimes wonder," he said to no one in particular, "whether or not Matthew Goff ever got around to learnin' the English language."

"Maybe he's a member of the Unknown Tongue," I said.

Wallace gave me a sour look. "Who's this?" he asked Subrinea.

"A friend," she said. "He's kind of a detective."

"Friend," said Chuck Wallace, without rancor, "you'd better watch your own tongue around these hills. Some folks don't take kindly to jokes about their religion."

"Sorry," I said, meaning it. He read the honesty in my voice and stuck out his hand. We got introduced all around, and he led us back to the

43

feed bin where he had found the body of Jesse Simpson.

"I never saw nothing like it, Miss Brown," he said. "I knew he was dead the minute I saw him. I mean, his hair was burnt off and he was as red as a lobster all over. At least, as all over as I could see. I felt for his pulse, and his skin was hot as a tin roof in July. I called for the emergency ambulance, but it was a waste of time."

"He was one of the gardeners?" I asked.

Wallace nodded. "Poor old Simpson was horse crazy. He used to be a jockey."

"How old was he?'

"You name it." He shrugged. "Sixty-five, seventy easy. He was already here workin' as a hot walker when I got here, and that was in forty-six."

"What's a hot walker?"

"When the horse comes back after a run, he's all sweated up. Somebody has to walk him around for a half an hour or so to cool him down. But you can't live on the money you make that way. A dollar or so per horse. So Simpson took up gardening on the side. He worked pretty cheap there, too. Colonel Brown always likes the grounds looking well groomed, so he put Jesse on. Every time he could get away from his gardening chores he was down here with the horses."

"What was he doing today?"

"The usual. Mixing the feed. Sometimes I'd let

him walk a colt. He didn't ride any more, not since he took a bad fall a couple of years back."

"Any relatives?"

"A wife," said Wallace. "Most of these backstretchmen, they stay single. But Simpson married a hill girl back before the war, and she set up a little shop to tailor-make dresses and did all right."

"Has anyone told her?"

A look of embarrassment came over Wallace's face. "I clean forgot," he said.

"Does she have a phone?" Charity asked.

"No."

"That idiot Goff," said Subrinea, "He'll blurt it out to her like the latest weather report."

"Do you know her?" asked Charity.

"She made this dress."

"Let's go," said my girl, "Loyal, we're taking your car."

The two girls went out the front door. We went back to the little office, and while Loyal talked with the local operator, I had a nip of good Kentucky J.T.S. Brown and branch water with Chuck Wallace. His hand was shaking as he poured the bourbon.

"I never saw nothing like that before," he repeated. "Burned red as a lobster, and not a mark on his overalls."

5

The Brown house was a mile up the hill from the stables. House wasn't the right word. It had tall white columns in front and looked like Tara in *Gone with the Wind*.

I admired the view. "What," I asked maliciously, "are you folks going to do if the AMA gets its way and outlaws cigarettes?"

"I reckon we'll have to secede from the Union again," said Loyal. He drove around to the rear of the house. "We save the front door for special occasions," he said, getting out. "Around these parts kitchen's the main room in the house, and Butterfield's no exception."

Three orange-red hound puppies came bursting out of the bushes and leaped up on him, yapping.

chil'n." To me, "I'm kind of their grandpappy. My hound, Blue, sired them."

The puppies sniffed me suspiciously. Deciding I was neither an enemy nor something to eat, they permitted me to scratch behind their soft, floppy ears.

An immensely fat Negro woman appeared at the door, wiping her hands on a dish towel.

"Mistah Loyal," she said with obvious delight. "You-all come to supper?"

"Sorry, Aunt Jenny," he said. "Just droppin' off some suitcases. This here's Mr. Ben Shock, from New York City. Ben, meet Aunt Jenny. She's the power behind the throne at Butterfield."

"Power behind the kitchen stove, you mean to say," Aunt Jenny wheezed, laughing. "You gentlemen have time for a cup of coffee?"

Loyal looked at me. I nodded. He said, "Just one, Aunt Jenny. Then we've got to get to town. There's a mess of trouble."

"That poor ole Mistah Simpson," she said, leading us inside. "This is sure going to break Miz Cora's heart. Although, between us and the gatepost, she's been a hoss-widder-lady ever since she married him."

In the huge kitchen, larger than an ordinary living room, a slim, pale-yellow boy who looked about twelve leaped up guiltily from the bowl of cake icing he had been sampling. Aunt Jenny grabbed him by one ear and ushered him toward

48

the back door. "John Henry," she said, "I tole you to keep your hungry mouth out'n my kitchen. Now you bring in this gentleman's luggage and put it in the main guest room."

"The big blue suitcase belongs to my partner," I said. "Miss Tucker."

Aunt Jenny gave me a flashing smile that Knew All. "And put that big blue one in the corner room Miss Subrinea's mammy used to have."

"Yes'm," said John Henry, unbothered by his ear-pulling. He dashed out as Aunt Jenny poured us two cups of the blackest coffee I'd ever seen. I happen to be a coffee cynic. I have searched all my life for the perfect cup of coffee. It has never been found. Certainly not in Aunt Jenny's sprawling kitchen. Her brew was as bitter as it was pungent and black.

Loyal laughed at my expression. "Aunt Jenny makes her coffee New Orleans style," he said. "Half chicory."

"Delicious," I lied gallantly.

That was a mistake. Beaming, Aunt Jenny filled my cup again. "Now, if you gentlemen will pardon me, I got to go upstairs and air them rooms out." She bustled out.

"I thought Lincoln freed the slaves," I said.

Loyal could have taken it wrong. He didn't. He laughed and said, "Aunt Jenny may own this house by now, for all I know. She's been here since Adger was a boy, and I understand her arrangement includes all kinds of mysterious and taxdodging payments in kind. Don't let her Aunt Jemima act fool you. There's a shrewd brain behind those sleepy eyes."

"Even so," I said recklessly, "certain black friends of mine would probably call her a handkerchief head."

Loyal smiled without humor. "Those friends," he said, "would end up with a whuppin' like their own mammy should have given them years ago. Aunt Jenny doesn't tolerate sass from anyone—man or woman, black or white. Your friends probably think Aunt Jenny's manner is degrading to herself and her race. Well, you just ought to hear what she has to say about black nationalists with their scraggly beards and dark glasses."

"Peace," I pleaded, holding up both hands.

He laughed and got up. "Let's talk business," he said, and rummaged in a cabinet. He came back with a bottle of amber liquid. "Apple brandy. Homemade, distilled from the finest cider ever pressed in these hills." He poured a generous slug into each cup of coffee. "That won't make it drinkable, but you won't care any more.

"Now," he went on, sitting down, "Subrinea asked you-all to come down because we felt that you'd look around with a fresh eye. Maybe you'd see something, maybe you wouldn't."

I sipped my rejuvenated brew and nodded.

"Now the game has changed. You got shot at. It looks like somebody murdered old Simpson, God knows why. Ben, here's where I have to talk turkey. Don't get mad at me."

I knew what was coming. "I won't."

"I had a check run on you. I used to be county attorney, and I've kept up my connections. You recently resigned from the New York City Police Force, but the word is that you got out just one step ahead of being fired."

"Half a step would be more like it," I admitted. "I had some strong enemies."

"My sources say you left to protect your friends on the force who would have tried to defend you and gotten in trouble themselves." He looked at me for an answer. I shrugged. What did he expect me to do? Haul out my Hero of the State medal and wave it around? "The only complaints I could find against you are that recently you've been shooting a little too straight and that you have the insane idea cops should be honest."

"Which," I said, "is why they invited me to resign three weeks ago."

Loyal sipped his coffee. "Now. The problem that brought you down here was Adger Brown's racetrack. Meanwhile, there've been two murder attempts, and one succeeded. We've got more than a simple case of community displeasure with the track." He got up and stood at the window, looking down over the rolling green hills crisscrossed with white wooden fences.

"This is my country," he said. "I grew up here and I'll die here. I love this place. And if it's sick, I want to make it well again. If we've got a rotten core somewhere, I want it cut out. No matter who it is, no matter who gets hurt." He turned. "Do you understand me, Ben?"

"If you can stick by it," I said. "But what happens when one of your best friends or even a relative comes up with his hand right in the middle of the till?"

"We've got a saying around these hills," he said. "When you're angry with someone you love, you're 'kindly mad.' Well, that's how I am now about Buckhorn County. I'm kindly mad and I want to get all the doubt and worries cleared up. Maybe, deep down, we're all still rednecks—but there's a streak of honesty in us too, Ben. I don't like to see that honesty pranked with."

"Who are we working for?"

He frowned. "I guess it'll have to be Butterfield Downs," he said. "We don't know how high this thing goes up. It might go as high as Louisville. If I got county credentials for you and Charity, it'd leak. As attorney for Butterfield, I'll put you on retainer as troubleshooters for the track. Adger Brown and I still pull a little weight around here, so that ought to be enough to keep you out of trouble for operating without a PI license."

"Right," I said. "We're not private investigators, we're troubleshooters."

Loyal laughed. "Tell it to the judge," he said.

6

We met the girls at Loyal's office and drove twelve miles up the Lexington Highway for dinner. Clean, white-painted farm buildings lined the road. In some fields horses grazed under the trees.

"How did she take it?" I asked. In the back seat, Blue whined.

Charity shook her head, swallowed hard enough for me to see, and looked away. "The first thing she did," she said, "was call the hospital and give them absolute instructions not to let an undertaker touch the body."

"That's the way it's still done in the hills," said Loyal. "The neighbor women will come over to help around the house. The neighbor men will wash and dry poor old Simpson and lay out the corpse. Then they'll have a sittin'-up."

"Sounds like a wake," I said.

"That's what it is," he said. "I'll have to go over, after the town meeting. Come along if you want."

Charity shuddered, but I said I would.

"Is the town meeting tonight?" Subrinea asked, brushing back her hair. She was uncommonly pretty. Charity noticed my approval and revived enough to pinch my arm until it stung.

"Eight o'clock at the new high school," said Loyal. "We'd better be there."

Subrinea swore in a manner unbecoming to one so young and beautiful. "Those mealy-mouthed bastards," she said. "They get together in a high school my daddy's money built to see if they can run him out of business."

Loyal shushed her as we turned off the highway into a lane that ran beside a lazy brown creek. The water was so still it looked like a dusty mirror.

"Ben," he asked, "have you ever eaten Kentucky catfish?"

"Nope."

"Eccch," said Charity.

"Now, there, Miss Tucker," he said lightly, "you're slandering our proudest dish. Some of those channel cats run four or five feet, and you can cut a steak off them just like a five-pound chunk of white meat from a turkey's breast. Then you deep-fry it in crumb batter and eat it with hush puppies."

"What's a hush puppy?" Charity asked suspiciously.

Subrinea laughed. "You'll see."

We did. Hush puppies, we discovered, were bread sticks made with corn meal, bits of fish, and onions, all deep-fried in the same grease that had cooked the catfish. I grazed my way through about ten pounds of catfish and hush puppies without coming up for air. With the meal we drank pitchers of ice-cold draft beer served out of a Budweiser cask.

Light-headed, I asked, "What the hell kind of beer is this? Doesn't taste like any Budweiser I've ever drunk."

Loyal grinned. "Uncle Jeff bought six of those casks in 1951 and he's been using them ever since. This is home brew. He makes it himself. Better than any store brand you can buy."

"The basic difference between Kentuckians and the rest of the country," I said, feeling profound, "is that Kentuckians know how to live off the land."

"That's the way we were brought up," agreed Loyal. "When I was a boy the only money you saw was when you sold the crop, and most of that went straight to the bank to pay off your seed loan and interest on the mortgage. Except for a couple of pairs of overalls and a few hooks to replace those you lost off your trot line, everything else came from the land."

"What's a trot line?" Charity asked.

"A line stretched across the creek with hooks every five or six feet. That's probably how this cat was caught."

"I thought trot lines were illegal," said Subrinea.

Boone laughed and waved for more of Uncle Jeff's home brew.

Shortly after seven, Boone called, "Uncle Jeff, what's the damage?"

Uncle Jeff, a tall, cadaverous Negro who must have been at least eighty years old, wandered over wiping his hands on a towel. "Let's see," he said, "You-all had four catfish orders with hush puppies and three pitchers of brew. Make that fo' dollars and a quartuh."

I beat Loyal and handed Uncle Jeff a five-dollar bill. He fished in his pocket, gave me back three quarters, and went away, humming. I got up, leaving the quarters on the tablecloth.

"Forgot your change," Loyal said.

"That's a tip."

He shook his head. "Uncle Jeff doesn't take tips. He's a proud man. Try to turn him into a beggar and he'll likely put ground glass in your next hush puppy."

Not wanting to ruin that fantastic meal with a shattered Bud bottle, I picked up my change and we went out to the car.

"One of these days," Loyal said, driving away, "progress is going to catch up with Uncle Jeff. He's going to get a neon sign and a juke box and start serving frozen fish, and then we're going to have to find us another catfish place."

The sun was just setting behind us as we turned onto the blacktop. It threw the Ford's shadow far ahead of us, like a dark finger pointing to the town of Gethsemane.

"How did your father come to build a high school?" Charity asked Subrinea.

"A lot of the walking boys and even some of the jockeys never finished school," Subrinea said. "Daddy tried to get the local school to accept them part time. They said they couldn't afford it. So Daddy built his own high school and then donated it to the town with the agreement that anyone who lived or worked at Butterfield could attend any classes they wanted."

"There are some of us who think a new school wasn't such a good idea," said Loyal. "You see, the only thing that differentiates these hill people, who don't have two dollars to rub together, from poor white trash—or, for that matter, your Northern welfare cases—is the hill man's tremendous pride. Individuality is a way of life around here, and some of us hate to see anything push these people toward conformity."

"If education is conformity, we need more conformity," Subrinea said hotly. "If those proud individualists had a little more education, maybe they'd *have* two dollars to rub together and wouldn't have to be so damned independently poor."

"Destroying the hill man's pride is fine if you replace it with a position in society. But if he stays a backwoodsman and loses his fierce pride in being one, he's nothing more than a welfare case sitting on a hill."

"You don't seem to think much of welfare," said Charity.

"No ma'am, I don't," said Loyal. "There's plenty of work to be done. If a man gets down on his luck and can't cut it, you surely don't want him or his family to go hungry. But what's wrong with letting him put in a day's work instead of going on the dole? As a matter of fact, most men around here would spit in your eye if you offered them welfare. They can always hunt and fish a little, and sell furs from a trap line to get a little cash money to buy sugar and salt."

"Those days are over, Loyal!" Subrinea almost shouted. "How can you sit there fat, dumb, and happy with your State College education and say that no one else ought to have one?"

"Hold on there, missy," he said. "I didn't say any such thing. I came down from the hills, and I'm proud of it. But nobody gave me anything. I scrambled for every day of college, and I had to beat out two good men to get my job as county attorney."

"Having Harmon Boone as a daddy didn't exactly hurt you any in this county," she snapped.

Loyal slammed on the brakes and skidded the car to a stop dead in the middle of the road.

"Subrinea," he said grimly, "you ever say something like that to me again and I'll put you over my knee and whop your tail until you sing for forgiveness. You know as well as I do that my daddy never showed up back from Mexico until I was already halfway through Kentucky State. My Aunt Cecelia never got one red penny from him all those years. I'm as much a hill boy as any Unknown Tongue living on Blood Mountain."

He looked at Charity and me. "I want to apologize to you folks for arguing family matters in front of you, but a man just can't let something like that go by."

"If you don't get moving," Subrinea said stiffly, "we're going to be late."

He started the car and we drove in silence to the high school. It was on the outskirts of town, a low, modern building. Behind it was a taller one, and around fifty cars were parked in the lot between the two.

"That's the school gym," said Loyal, glancing at Subrinea. "We had us some pretty good basketball games there last year." Subrinea sniffed. She wasn't buying his oblique peace offer.

Inside, a hundred or so folding chairs were arranged in rows facing a small stage at one end of the auditorium. There were painted basketball lines on the wooden floor, and a basketball hoop hung at each end of the room—one directly over the stage itself.

We mingled for a few minutes, meeting blue-overalled men who all seemed to be named Jed or Adam or Will. Their faces were hard, deeply lined. Quick to smile and laugh, they had cold blue eyes that never appeared to blink.

Six gloomy-faced men filed out onto the stage and sat on folding chairs. A seventh came forward. He was thin and gangly, and wore a black frock coat.

"That's Oppie Hornbuckle, the Mayor," whispered Subrinea.

The Mayor called the meeting to order, and for half an hour there was spirited arguing and voting on such vital issues as the status of the town clerk (who wanted a ten-dollar-a-month raise) and the decision to register a complaint with the Argo Hand Laundry for allegedly polluting Silver Creek with detergents.

"Now, brethren and sisters," said Hornbuckle, "we have a report from Counselor Loyal Boone in regard to the Butterfield race track. As you know, the Town Council has expressed worries about the nature of the visitors this track might bring here. Gamblers, touts, and fancy women may get lost in the crowd in a big city like Louisville, but the citizens of Gethsemane have a right to know what effect these foreigners may have on our way of life. I am sure we will all listen to Counelor Boone with great interest."

He sat down. Loyal leaped up on the stage and jammed both hands on his hips.

"His Honor the Mayor," he said, "may have

the words, but he doesn't have the tune. Butterfield Downs isn't going to hurt Gethsemane—Butterfield Downs is going to *save* Gethsemane! Horsemen and horseplayers aren't any different than you and me except in one way—they got more money. And Colonel Brown's track is going to bring more of that money into this community than you ever dreamed existed."

Mayor Hornbuckle stood up. "The purpose of your appearance is to give us a progress report," he drawled, "not to speechify all night."

"My humble apologies," Loyal said bowing deeply. "Since His Honor was speechifying, I thought it was safe for me to do likewise." He turned back to the audience.

"As you all know, Colonel Brown is presently in the Lexington Hospital, suffering from a minor heart seizure. But the doctors say he's going to be all right, and for that we are truly grateful. I'll speak for him tonight. In the past two months we have spent slightly over one hundred thousand dollars on track construction. Forty-one thousand went for supplies and the rest went for labor. With the exception of a state engineer who supervised the wiring, all of that money was paid to residents of Buckhorn County. Most of you set your tables tonight with money from Butterfield Downs."

Hornbuckle stood up again, but before he could speak, Loyal waved his hand and said, "All right, Mayor, no speechifying." He took out a slip of paper and, consulting it, said, "Things are goin' slower than we hoped. We originally planned to be ready for a fall meet. Now it looks like we'll have to delay until next April."

As if to punctuate his words, a flash of lightning flared through the auditorium and a clap of thunder shook the building. When the sound died down, a stocky man with a bushy white mane of hair was on his feet, demanding the floor.

"If the speaker please," called the man, "may I be recognized."

Loyal nodded. "It's a pleasure to recognize the distinguished State Senator, the Honorable Osgood Treffit."

"I have only one question to ask the speaker," said Treffit. "You all know my record. I have represented the good people of Buckhorn County in the State Senate for over twenty years. I have kept our faith in the Word and fought to keep outsiders from destroying our Garden of Eden in the wilderness. I—"

"We are all familiar with the Senator's accomplishments," Boone said dryly. "What's the question?"

"All right. By what right, by what dictate of Satan, by what self-serving mandate of greed does Colonel Adger Brown *dare* sully our little community with a brazen temple of gambling and

64

sin? Has the Almighty Dollar replaced the Almighty God? Has—"

"Since when," shouted Subrinea, leaping up, "has Osgood Treffit gone into partnership with God?"

"Young woman," rumbled the Senator, "you are speaking to an elder."

"Hoo-ha!" said Subrinea. "Your halo is a little tarnished, Senator. Have you forgotten who opened the first tavern in Gethsemane? His initials were O. T. Who sold what was supposed to be fertile bottomland to that boys' club from Chattanooga, only it turned out to be under water seven months out of the year? Who said a tithe for the First Baptist Church was Communism and refused to go to services for a year until the donation was made voluntary?"

Lightning flickered and thunder roared again. The heavens were coming in right on cue.

Mayor Hornbuckle was on his feet pounding his gavel for order. "There will be no personal attacks in this meeting!"

"No, no," persisted the Senator, "I'll answer this young woman." He turned back to Subrinea. "My conduct is not under question here, Miss Brown. The question is whether or not this community should wait passively for a deluge of undesirables and criminals to flock to our peaceful valley."

"Isn't it a little late for that, Senator?" asked

Loyal. "The State Racing Commission authorized Butterfield Downs two years ago."

"A midnight bill, slipped past an unsuspecting Senate in the dead of night!" answered Treffit.

"*You* voted for it," said Loyal. He looked around at his neighbors. "Don't any of you wonder what's happening here? You all knew about this track years ago, and most of you were happy as a possum swinging from a beechnut tree. It brought money into the area, it put meat on your tables. Now all of a sudden you're wondering if you made the right choice. Well, friends, you really don't have much to say about it. Colonel Brown's property doesn't even lie within Gethsemane Township. We want to be good neighbors, but don't push us too far. I can tell you honestly, if we have to bring in outsiders to finish the work, we will."

"Perhaps the Township limits might be extended," called Senator Treffit.

"Order!" shouted the Mayor. "Counselor, Senator, let's stop this senseless name-calling and threatening. We all agree that if Colonel Brown wants to open a racetrack on his own property, that's his right and privilege. All we ask is that he consider the greater good of the community as well."

"Mayor," Loyal said, "no man in Buckhorn County has done so much for this community as Colonel Brown. He built this high school. He put a wing on the hospital. He's been raising thoroughbreds at Butterfield for more than twenty-five years. He's been a good neighbor. That's why I find it hard to understand what's happening now."

"You tell him, Loyal!" shouted one of the overalled men in the audience.

Another man stood up. "That goes for me and mine too," he said. "I vow there isn't a better man or a more honest one in this state than Colonel Brown. With all due respect, Mayor Hornbuckle and Senator Treffit ain't speaking for *my* kin." He sat down and his mouth worked tightly over a cud of tobacco.

"We're not *getting* anywhere," protested the Mayor. He raised his gavel, but before he could pound it again the lights flickered and went out. At the same moment a bolt of lightning rent the sky and thunder clapped, making the auditorium seem blacker than ever. The people murmured in the way people do when they have been removed from the world's reality. I heard a voice that sounded like Hornbuckle's shouting, "Turn on the emergency lighting." Another voice called, "We ain't got no emergency lighting." A third shouted, "Anybody got a flashlight?"

Then came a slow, deliberate tapping on the hard wood of the floor. It moved through the darkness, each tap echoing hollowly against the walls. Near me, someone sucked in his breath. The deliberate tapping continued, and then there came a hollower thump as some hard object struck the stage apron.

For a moment it was as if the world held its breath. The murmur in the room had ceased. From the darkness near the stage a quiet voice began to speak. Without being loud or dramatic, it dominated the auditorium.

"And these signs shall follow them that believe," it said.

"In my name shall they cast out devils; they shall speak with new tongues; they shall take up serpents; and if they drink any deadly thing, it shall not hurt them; they shall lay hands on the sick, and they shall recover."

An almost soundless gasp rippled through the room.

The voice raised to full volume.

"LET THERE BE LIGHT."

The lightning flickered again and the lights flashed on. A tall, hawk-faced man stood in front of the stage. He wore tattered black trousers and a long black frock coat that had seen better days. A huge-brimmed hat shaded his eyes, which stared straight ahead from the crags of his face.

Subrinea squeezed my arm. "It's Blind Judd," she whispered.

"Nice trick," I said. "One of his buddies throws the main switch, then puts it on again when the boss calls for light."

"Shhhh," said a man behind me.

Blind Judd raised both hands toward the ceiling. "Let us have light," he repeated, "for ordinary mortals are blind without it. Their eyes do not look inward toward the soul, but outward toward evil and material things. Confess your sins, lest you find yourself at the throne of God and speechless before your Master. His eye is on the sparrow, and I know he watches me. Prepare for the day of doom. Judgment Day is at hand."

"Oh, brother," said Charity.

"God is not mocked!" Blind Judd shouted. "Whatsoever a man soweth, that shall he also reap."

"Why doesn't somebody stop him?" I asked. "Who the hell is he?"

"He's the leader of the Blood Mountain sect of the Unknown Tongue," said Subrinea.

"Silence!" roared Blind Judd. "I hear the voice of the Whore of Babylon. Beware, sinners! Shall Gethsemane be destroyed with fire and brimstone because of this one's shame? Missy Brown, what will you do in Heaven for whiskey and tobacco? Will you wager on the Angel's wings? Will you cast dice with the Lord? No, Missy, you will fall! You will plunge, calling for mercy, into the lake of fire and brimstone that surrounds the domain of hell. You will swim for eternity among scorpions and serpents." His finger, as if guided by some supernatural power, found and pointed directly at Subrinea. I felt a chill rising among my back muscles.

"Good people of Gethsemane, cast out the

whore. Get right with God before it's too late. Wrestle the Devil with prayer! Confess your sins before men and roll away the burden that traps Jesus in the cave of your transgressions. Exile this woman and the abomination her kind would bring to our land. The Lord is knocking at your heart, and the Devil is waiting to see if you will answer and let Him in. Remember, sinners, tomorrow's sun may never rise. This may be your last chance to take God's offer of a home in Glory! Banish her! Banish her father! Banish the evil of gambling and drink and wenching they would corrupt you with. Brethren and sisters, cut the last rotten speck out of this good apple of Gethsemane!"

The lightning and thunder came in to punctuate his words. The lights went out again, and this time the women in the crowd squealed in fright. The methodical tapping continued down the aisle, and the great entrance door creaked open and then slammed shut.

There was a silence that seemed to go on forever. Then, next to me, a woman began sobbing. When I realized it was Subrinea, I put my arm around her. She clutched at me and I felt hot tears on the back of my hand.

The lights came on. Charity looked at Subrinea cuddling up to me, started to bridle, then saw the tears and put her own arm around her friend. I disentangled myself and started down the aisle toward Loyal.

Up on the stage, Mayor Hornbuckle pounded his gavel and shouted, "This meeting is adjourned!" He slammed the gavel again and then glared at Loyal. "We never had trouble like this before you started your goddamned racing track."

Boone ignored him and we went back to the girls. Subrinea caught him by the hand.

"Loyal," she said, still crying, "I'm scared. Blind Judd was like a death token."

"It looks like my speech about hill individuality came back and bit me on the hand," he said. "Subrinea, I'm sorry. Don't pay him no mind."

"It's Daddy," she whispered. "I just know something's happened to him. Loyal, call Lexington, please. I'm *scared.*"

We got out of there and drove to a small roadside tavern. Loyal fed quarters and dimes into the pay telephone while the rest of us sipped nervously on bottles of genuine Budweiser. It didn't have the kick of Uncle Jeff's.

Loyal came back. He smiled and touched Subrinea's hair.

"Everything's fine, honey," he said. "The Colonel's resting quietly, and he had a good day. Even got up and watched TV this afternoon."

She sighed deeply and snuggled back against him. He reached over her, picked up his beer, and drank deeply from it. I began to feel sloppily sentimental and got my hand around Charity's waist.

"I called Chuck Wallace to come out and get you girls," Loyal said, "I need the car to take Ben out to Cora Simpson's for the sittin'-up."

I had forgotten the Kentucky wake. It wasn't exactly what I'd been working myself up to for the rest of the evening. But I knew I had to talk with the widow.

I sighed and sipped at my beer. It tasted flat. In about ten minutes Chuck Wallace arrived, and the girls piled into his station wagon. I got into Loyal's Ford and we started up the hill to the Simpson place.

7

Loyal turned off the blacktop and we found ourselves on a dirt road. Deep ruts had been worn on both sides of a center ridge that threatened to rip off our oil pan. Several times we actually hit bottom and heard the grinding scrape of red earth against the underside of the car. Both sides of the narrow road dropped off to axle-shattering ditches.

"You really need a jeep to get up this damned road," Loyal grumbled. "But nobody can afford one. Do you know a jeep runs over four thousand dollars these days?"

I didn't. The last time I had ridden in a jeep it was painted olive drab with a white star on the hood. The windshield had been folded down over the hood so as not to offer a glaring target to Viet Cong snipers.

Listening to the road hump banging against Loyal's oil pan, I shuddered and felt grateful that my Fleetwood wasn't clawing its way up this latter-day Burma Road.

The Simpson place was easy to find. Cars were parked beside the ditch for a quarter of a mile before we reached it. As we got closer, the noise that filled the quiet night air sounded more like a party than a wake.

The house, an unpainted shack with a front porch perched on stilts, leaned precariously to the right. There were no shades on the windows, and dark shadows flickered across the panes as the people inside moved in front of the kerosene light.

"I should have parked back there," said Loyal. "Get out, I'll go on up the road a piece."

I piled out and stood by the side of the weatherbeaten road while the Ford disappeared around a curve. Two men came out of the bushes and approached me.

"Howdy," said one.

"Howdy," I said. It came out sounding like Brooklyn.

"Friend of the dead?" the other asked.

"I'm a friend of the Browns. Mr. Simpson worked for them."

"That he did," said the first man. "God bless you, stranger, for paying respect to the dead."

"Jesse Simpson was a good man," said the second man. "He never put bow to a fiddle that he didn't make every bird in the bushes come over to listen to the way music ought to sound."

"He knew his time was coming, Jesse did," said the first man. "Do you know he laid in four barrels of salt to pack his grave? He'll rest as sweet and fresh as a slab of pork until the Judgment Day."

"There ain't many like Jesse left," mourned the other man. "The young'uns are all taking up the city ways. It's a sin, the way they plunk a body in the earth without no sittin'-up, and when the anniversary comes around next year, you can bank there won't be no funeralizing. Put the bones in the ground and forget them by Sunday, that's the new way."

"It's a sinful way," said the first man, looking to me for confirmation.

"Amen," I said.

"Now that we talked of the dead," said the first of my new friends, "I reckon it'd be proper if we swigged some from the jug. Try this, neighbor. It's four-day-old corn, run off right from the top of the mash."

I took the heavy stone jug and held it in both hands. It weighed around ten pounds. I gulped some of the liquid, slopping it down my chin.

"Wow," I tried to say. Nothing came out but a husky wheeze.

The first man hooked one finger through the jug, tossed it up on his shoulder, twisted his head, and poured a stream of liquid into his mouth. He swallowed it, gave a contented "Ahhhh," put down the jug, and wiped his mouth with his sleeve.

"That's good shine," said the other man. "First good I've had this year."

"It's the corn," said the first man. "I always use top-grade eatin' corn, not feed corn like some folks do."

"Quality makes the difference," I croaked.

The men laughed and one of them gave me a healthy swat on the back with a work-toughened hand that felt like a brick. It brought my breath back and I recovered sufficiently to reach out for the stone jug again. A hand beat me to it: Loyal's.

He took a healthy swig and, to my admiration, spoke without choking. "See you boys have met my friend, Ben. This is Jake and Ezra Morgan. They're corn farmers."

The first man cackled. "Corn farmers. That's a good 'un, Loyal. I got to remember that one."

"See you later," said Loyal, drawing me toward the ramshackle porch. In an undertone, he said, "One drink of that white lightning is an experience. Two drinks are insanity."

We climbed the rickety steps and tapped on the hinge-sprung door. There was no doorknob—just a strip of leather hanging out around a hole. When someone lifted the latch inside, the strip lengthened.

"Howdy, Sister Bessie," said Loyal to the drab,

heavyset woman who had opened the door. "We come to pay our respects."

"Hmmmmph," said Sister Bessie, unimpressed. She let us in, then headed silently for another room.

It was oppressively hot. I could smell the oily aroma of burning kerosene, and another sweetish scent that took me back to Vietnam. Somebody hadn't salted Jesse Simpson down well enough.

The room was empty except for a small center table on which three kerosene lamps burned and smoked. Against the far wall two chairs supported a rude wooden coffin. The lid leaned against the corner.

Loyal must have noticed my nose wrinkle. "Don't let on," he whispered. "Just go over and bow your head and then we'll get out."

Jesse Simpson was even more fragrant when we stood over him. He lay peacefully on the raw wood of the pine box. His hands, crossed over his chest, glowed redly in the lamplight. Someone had tried to powder down his ruddy face. That was a mistake. Now he looked like a ninety-year-old Kabuki dancer. His eyes were weighted down with two nickels. On one the Indian faced up; the other showed the buffalo. I couldn't remember how long it had been since I last saw an Indian-head nickel. I felt an irreverent urge to turn the buffalo nickel over so it matched the Indian head. Loyal drew me away toward the kitchen. I realized I had been holding my breath, and exhaled noisily.

The kitchen was jammed full of people. Just as we stepped inside, someone began singing a hymn, and in seconds everyone had chimed in. I didn't know the words, so I just stood there.

> Where will you spend eternity?
> The question comes to you and me.
> Tell me, what shall your answer be?
> Where will you spend eternity?

I gave Loyal a surreptitious glance. He had his head back and was singing as loud as anyone. I sidled over into the corner and tried to look appreciative as the singers roared on.

> Leaving the straight and narrow way,
> Going the downward road today,
> Sad will their final ending be,
> Lost through a long eternity.

I thought it was over, but the volume increased as everyone belted out,

> *Eternity! Eternity!*
> Lost through a long eternity.
> Repent, believe this very hour.
> Trust in the Saviour's grace and
>   power,
> Then will your joyous answer be
> *Saved through a long eternity!*

The final refrain rattled the rafters. Most of the women were crying as they sang, and the men were sharing another bilious-looking stone jug.

I looked at the rite as if from a great distance, and then I thought, Who the hell are *you*, Benjamin Lincoln Shock, to stand aloof and sneering among these deeply reverent and impassioned people? A wave of shame swept over me, and I felt like crawling into the pine box alongside poor old Jesse Simpson. Whether or not I understood what these people were doing, it was their way of life and death, and what better did I have to offer?

My turmoil must have showed on my face. Loyal held out the stone jug. "Here," he said, "you got one more swig coming. This is sittin'-up shine; it's been cut with branch water."

Cut or not, it closed up my windpipe as efficiently as the Morgan brothers' brew had outside. I choked my thanks.

Loyal took me into a third room. It was filled with women, all sitting in a circle, sewing on a large cloth object that I recognized as a patchwork quilt. They were humming quietly among themselves. First one woman would raise her voice a little to state a melody; then the others would come in and harmonize. The melody seemed to circle the little group from right to left.

In the farthest corner, a slim, dark figure sat. At first I thought it was a young girl, draped in a heavy black veil. When we went over and she looked up, I saw how wrong I had been. This was Cora Simpson, and she was at least sixty.

The soft lamplight and an expression of intense purity had combined to make her face look like a girl's.

"Miz Simpson," said Loyal, "I'm grieved for your trouble."

"Thank you kindly, Mr. Boone," she said. "It's the Lord's will."

"This is my friend, Ben Shock," he said. "He's working with us out at Butterfield."

She held out a white claw of a hand. I took it. It was cold and trembling.

"Mighty proud to meet you," Cora Simpson said.

"Mrs. Simpson," I said, "I hate to intrude at this time. But if you could answer a few questions?"

"No bother a-tall," she said. "You're a Yankee boy, aren't you?"

"Yes, ma'am."

"I could tell. I heard voices like yourn on the TV. Where up there are you from?"

"New York," I said.

"Jesse went to New York once," she said. "He rid at a big track called Saratoga."

"Mrs. Simpson," I said, "was Jesse worried about anything lately? Did he mention anything unusual?"

"Nary a thing," she said. "He had a mite of kidney trouble this last winter, kept him up nights."

"Nothing about his job?"

"Nary a word." She frowned. "Mr. Boone?"

"Yes, Miz Simpson?"

"That Sheriff Goff. He came over and told me I was breaking the law by taking Jesse away from that hospital. He said I was supposed to leave Jesse there and let him cut him open so they could find out what killed him."

Loyal muttered under his breath, then said aloud, "I'll talk to him."

"I told him I'd already sent my yarb doctor over and he talked with those city doctors and they reached an agreement. So I brought my man home. Well, Sheriff Goff, he up and said he would get an injunction to keep us from going on with the buryin', and I got my dander up then."

Loyal signed. "What did you do, Miz Simpson?"

She smiled behind her veil, and for a moment I was looking back through another veil, that of time, to the iron-hard men who followed Daniel Boone into these hills. "I told him that if he come within a country mile of this house, my cousins from Hootin' Holler would put a rifle ball right between his eyes." She chuckled a little. "He took on something fierce, but he ain't been back."

Loyal pressed her hands between his own. "Don't you worry none," he said. "I'll straighten things out. And you go on with your buryin'. The sheriff won't bother you."

As he straightened, she reached under the

81

chair and took up a small brown notebook. "Mr. Boone, I hate to trouble you, but my Jesse, he never turned in his time for this week. And we're a mite short, what with the coffin and the store-bought clothes and everything."

Loyal took the notebook. He dug in his pocket and came up with a wad of money. He counted it, handed it to her. "Here's forty dollars on account," he said. "I'll go over Jesse's figures and bring the rest out tomorrow. And then there's the pension payment. Don't worry about a thing, Miz Simpson."

The bills crumpled in the thin, white fingers. "God bless ye, Mr. Boone," she said tonelessly.

We went down the back steps and walked around the house to the road.

"Excuse me, individualistic, independent hill man," I said. "Since when does an old retainer like Simpson make forty bucks for a couple of days work tending grass?"

"I don't know *what* we owe him," he said defensively. "I'll have to work it out with the bookkeeper."

"Along with the pension payment? Five gets you ten that Butterfield never paid a dime into any pension fund since the day it began. Why don't you admit it? You're going to break all your own rules and give that woman charity."

"She won't know it," he said.

We turned up the bumpy road toward his car. After a while he said, "She's an old woman, Ben.

I seen them before when they're this old. The life'll go out of her. She won't go down to her dress shop any more, or if she does she'll be dreamy and slow and lose all her customers. She'll spend all her time thinking about her laying-out dress, and what kind of coffin she's going to have."

"There are agencies to help people like her."

"The county farm?" He spat. "That'd kill her off in six weeks. Ben, I like you, but you're climbing my fences."

I didn't say any more. We got in the car. He put the notebook on the dashboard, and it fell open, revealing a pressed leaf.

I picked it up. It looked like a dried poinsettia leaf.

As Loyal started the engine, the rain began to fall.

8

God's Legions were marching across the heavens in full force, shooting off their cannons with violent flashes and mighty roars. The rain sheeted against the windshield as we turned off the blacktop. The night shadows crowded close in on us, then retreated at each flash of lightning.

The water was running down the road like a canal.

"This is a real cloudburst," Loyal said. "It'll wipe out some of those hill farmers who were there tonight."

"How?"

"By washing their topsoil down the mountain. And crops right along with it."

"Sounds like a hell of a way to make a living."

We pulled around to the back of the Brown

house. The big Fleetwood was parked there, looking none the worse for wear.

"Looks like Jim Hurley got your car fixed," said Loyal. We got out and ran. It was only ten yards or so to the back door, but we both arrived drenched.

Subrinea met us.

"Coats and shoes off," she said, holding out two big towels. "I'm not going to have any summer pneumonia around my house."

I mopped my dripping head, kicked off my shoes, and draped my wet jacket over a coat hook. I went over and sat down at the big kitchen table with Charity. Loyal and Subrinea joined us in a minute.

"Coffee's on," said Subrinea. I must have groaned a little because she grinned and said, "*My* coffee, not Aunt Jenny's."

"How was the wake?" asked Charity.

I told her.

"That poor woman," she said.

"What's a yarb doctor?" I asked Loyal.

"Why?"

"Mrs. Simpson said she sent her yarb doctor over to talk with the hospital doctors."

He nodded. "In hill talk that means herb. Yarb doctors claim there's a weed growing on Blood Mountain for every illness a body can get. The hill people swear by yarb doctors. Most of them won't even let a city doctor touch them."

"That must be fun for some poor hill kid with acute appendicitis," I said.

Subrinea poured our coffee. "I can't speak for or against yarb doctoring," Loyal answered. "But I have to admit that it seems to work. Miz Simmons' yarb doctor is an old darky named Uncle Uglybird McGee."

Charity choked.

"He's the son of a slave who was owned by the McGee family, over in Poke Hollow. All of those darkies are Uncle something-or-other. No one's sure how Uncle Uglybird picked up his name, but he's just about the ugliest man in the county, so it fits."

I sipped the coffee. It was delicious. Dark, hearty, without a trace of bitterness.

"Miss Brown," I said, "this is the first good cup of coffee I have had since my mammy went to Glory. May I have your hand in marriage?"

"Thank you kindly, sir," she said, curtsying, "but I am already bespoke." She fluttered her eyelashes at Loyal. It looked like the feud was over.

"I'll hand you," Charity muttered at me. Then, to Loyal, "Go on."

"Well," he said, sipping his own coffee, "a yarb doctor'll give you calamus root to chew for high blood pressure. Or sassafrilla tonic for the blood. Snakeroot is the mountaineers' aspirin. They boil the roots and use the liquid for chills and fevers. If a man cuts himself, the yarb doctor uses chimney soot to stop the bleeding. For old people with rheumatism they smear on groundhog grease."

"Do these remedies actually work?" Charity asked.

Loyal shrugged. "How often do a city doctor's remedies work?"

"Maybe half the time," I said. "Doctors have a saying: 'I treated the patient, but the Lord cured him.' "

"That's true in the hills, too. Yarb doctoring is pretty close to faith healing. It works as often as not."

"And those hospital doctors actually talk with Uncle Uglybird? They don't sound like the doctors I know."

"It's different down here," he said. "There aren't enough doctors to go around, even if the hill people would use them. So the professional doctors try to open up lines of communication through the yarb doctors. Sometimes they even call them in for consultation, especially if someone thinks he's been witched. And it works the other way, too. It may be a vicious rumor, but it's been said that Uncle Uglybird carries around a few ampules of penicillin packed in with his snakeroot."

"Who exactly," said Charity, "is that strange man, Blind Judd?"

Loyal got up and poured himself another half

cup of coffee. "There's nothing new about the Unknown Tongue," he said. "It's just one of many fundamentalist religious sects that have existed in these hills since pre-Civil War days."

"Why are they called Unknown Tongue?"

"Because when one of their services reaches a climax, with everybody hooting and hollering, they lapse into unintelligible speech that no one can understand, not even themselves."

"Mass hysteria," said Charity. "Self-induced hypnosis."

"Maybe," said Loyal. "But it comes right out of the Bible: 'They shall speak with new tongues; they shall take up serpents; and if they drink any deadly thing, it shall not hurt them!'"

"That's what Blind Judd said tonight," Charity said.

"Book of Mark," said Loyal Boone.

"Do they really handle snakes?"

"On special occasions. You see, Charity, in the hills the serpent represents the Devil. So it's part of the Unknown Tongue religion that they can tempt Satan and be protected by the Lord."

"Does the Lord come through for them?" I asked.

"Oh, they get bitten. But so far as I know, not a single Unknown Tongue has ever died from snakebite. And that includes rattlers, copperheads, and cottonmouths."

"Where does Blind Judd come in?" I prodded.

"Until a few years ago, the Unknown Tongue

had a preacher named Brother Randolph. He was a moderate man, for a fundamentalist. He'd come down out of the hills and preach sin and damnation, but then he'd sit down and have a drink with you. He vanished three or four years back, and Blind Judd—who seems to have appeared from nowhere—took over. He's enflamed most of the congregation against lowland sinmongers. There used to be a certain amount of interchange between us and them. Now they stay in their own community, and in the last year or so it hasn't been too safe for flatlanders to go hunting up in those hills."

"I can see what you mean," I said, "if it was an Unknown Tongue who used my Fleetwood for target practice."

He shook his head. "No one's been shot. But over a period of two years, three of our men have gone hunting and never come back. When we found them, they were dead from snakebite."

Charity shuddered. "Do you suspect the Unknown Tongue?"

"Some people do. I think it was just a run of bad luck. It's easy enough to get snakebit around here without blaming it on human manipulation. But a lot of folks are scared silly of the Unknown Tongue. And Blind Judd doesn't ease things up any, putting on exhibitions like he did tonight."

"Is he for real?" Charity asked.

"You mean, does he believe all that fire and brimstone stuff? Absolutely. Blind Judd's purpose in life is to save sinners, if he has to kill them to do it."

"I," announced Subrinea, "have had enough of this talk. I'll have nightmares as it is."

Loyal looked at his watch. "Reckon you're right. It's after eleven."

"My God," said Charity. "Ben, do you realize it's been less than eight hours since I saw that damned crow explode?"

"Don't remind me," I said.

Loyal got back into his damp jacket. Subrinea handed him an umbrella. He bent over and kissed her.

"Don't worry about a thing, pumpkin," he said. "Everything's going to be all right."

It was still raining as hard as ever. He got in the car, started it, and as he drove past the kitchen door, tossed back the umbrella. Subrinea caught it and waved goodbye.

"You've got quite a fellow," Charity said.

Subrinea smiled. "I think so too."

We lazed around the kitchen for another few minutes. Then, yawning, I said good night and went up to my room. John Henry had unpacked me neatly. I spent a few minutes down the hall in the bathroom, and as I padded back to my room I met Charity, swathed in a plaid bathrobe. She wore flat sandals, and the top of her head only came to my chin.

I tilted her head up and kissed the tip of her nose.

"Good night, baby," I said.

She didn't say anything. I gave her behind a gentle swat and went back to my room as she closed the bathroom door.

The heavenly army was still marching around bashing its drums and shooting off its cannons. The rain drummed against the windowpane and gusts of wind shook the glass.

I stripped down to my boxer shorts and slid under the thin sheet. It was pleasantly cool in the room, but the air was humid. I put both hands behind my head and stared at the ceiling. When the lightning flashed, dark shadows flooded through the room, ebbing just as quickly when the flare died.

Well, what are you doing. Ben old man?

Are you starting to get over not being a cop anymore? Is this insane gypsy life of yours going to work? Are you going to operate as a complete human being again?"

I didn't know.

Okay, down to work.

What killed Jesse Simpson?

What about all those snakebitten hunters? Do they tie in with the copperhead Adger Brown found in his bed?

Why had Gethsemane turned on Brown and his racetrack so suddenly?

Yes, our work was cut out for us.

The lightning flared, and I flirted with the edges of sleep.

The door opened.

A quiet figure slipped inside. The door closed softly. The bed sagged under a weight.

"If you're Blind Judd," I mumbled, "I've already been saved."

Clothing rustled and swished to the floor. Warm flesh pressed up against me.

"Sorry, lady," I said, "but I'm bespoke."

The lightning flared. I saw Charity's face close to mine. Her eyes were moist.

"Ben," she said in a little girl's voice, "I'm scared of the thunder."

I hugged her. I wasn't sure this was such a good idea. The night we first met, Charity had been pinned under the squirming body of a Riverside Park rapist. When he pulled a gun on me, I blew the bastard's brains out. It was messy, and Charity caught most of the mess. Since then, as close as we had become, that man's degenerate dead body had always been between us. We both hoped that time would make things right. So far it hadn't.

"Ben," she said, "do you think there's really a plot against Butterfield Downs?"

"Something's going on," I said. She tickled my chest. I slapped her hand.

"Could be the Mayor and the good Senator are angling for a payoff," she said. "Maybe everything else is just coincidence."

"It wasn't coincidence that shot at us."

"You said it yourself: some hill moonshiner who thought we were revenue agents."

"Jesse Simpson?"

"Who knows? Some strange kind of stroke? Maybe he drank wood alcohol."

"What are you getting at?"

"If we aren't needed here, Ben, we could keep going. To Mexico, or Guatemala. Maybe things would be better there."

I shook my head in the darkness. "I'm not very smart, baby, but I know this much: You can't get away from something you carry inside you. If anything, it only magnifies itself the further you get from home."

We didn't say anything for a while. The rain banged on the window.

She sighed. I didn't have to say any more. There wasn't any way out for us. We were committed.

We kissed each other for a while, little nibbling kisses, then deep, searching ones. Her breath caught in her throat as I touched her.

"Oh, Ben," she whispered, "I love you so."

We kicked the sheet aside and our skimpy clothes with it, and as the lightning flashed against the ceiling and the thunder marched up and down the hills, we tried to erase the ghost between us.

For a breathless moment I thought it was going to happen. But then she stiffened and began to cry. I tried to pull away, but she clutched at me. Still, it was no good and we both knew it.

I touched her cheek. It was wet with tears.

"Ben, Ben," she whispered, "I'm sorry."

"Don't worry, baby," I said. I held her close. She shuddered, but then she came into my arms and lay quietly against my chest. Her lips moved silently. I knew what they were saying. "Sorry . . . sorry."

She sobbed for a while. Then she slept.

It was a long time before I did.

9

When I was awakened by a symphony of blue jays perched outside my window, the sunlight was streaming in and Charity was gone. The thunder of the previous night was only a dim memory as I meandered downstairs in search of coffee.

It was only a few minutes before eight, but I was wide awake. Aunt Jenny looked up from the stove as I entered the kitchen.

"Morning, Mr. Ben," she said. "Can I get you some coffee?"

I said yes and prayed that she had gone a little lighter on the chicory this morning.

Whoever runs that Great Coffee Percolator in the Sky wasn't listening. If anything, Aunt Jenny's brew was even stronger. Still, it was hot.

Manfully I sipped it and asked, "Have you seen Miss Tucker this morning?"

"She went out a little while ago with Miss Subrinea," said Aunt Jenny. "Can I fry you some eggs?"

"If you don't mind," I said. "Scrambled is fine."

"Mind? Shoo, that's my work, Mr. Ben." She put a heavy black skillet on the electric stove, and soon a couple of eggs were sizzling in melted butter.

The door banged open and Charity came in, followed by Subrinea.

"Good morning," said my girl. "Sleep well?"

"Like a log," I said. Maybe we took Subrinea in; maybe we didn't. She poured herself a cup of Aunt Jenny's brew and joined me at the table. Charity fluttered around the room, trying to make herself useful and only getting in the way. Finally I said, "Save the energy, baby. You may need it later."

"You both will," said Subrinea. "We're all going riding after you have breakfast."

"Riding? Where? And on what?"

"I'll give you the grand tour of Butterfield," she said. "And on horses."

I shook my head. "Not me. Horseback riding is for young people with springs for muscles. Old age and infirmity have taken me out of that scene."

"Please come, Ben," said Charity. "It'll be fun,

98

and we do want to look around the farm."

"The two of you go," I said. "I will meanwhile sit here and toast my chilly toes at the fire, and maybe later I'll get hold of Loyal and talk a few things over."

"Oh, he's here now," said Subrinea.

"Where?"

"Up at the track."

"Good. I'll go up there after breakfast. In," I added, "my trusty Fleetwood."

"All right," she said, half miffed. I couldn't help it. The last thing anyone in Kentucky was going to see was Benjamin Lincoln Shock on a horse.

"Let's all meet back here around noon for lunch," suggested Subrinea. "We'll compare notes and decide where to go next."

"Good enough," I said, devoting myself to the scrambled eggs. Aunt Jenny, bless her, poured out another cup of coffee without being asked. I sipped at it dutifully as the girls left.

"Aunt Jenny," I said, "these eggs are marvelous."

She beamed, and as soon as she left the room I made a fast getaway. The keys were in the Fleetwood. The engine started easily, and, if anything, sounded even smoother than before it had taken the bullet in the radiator. I wondered what the mechanic had thought when he opened up the hood and found the 605-cubic-inch Whirlwind engine with dual racing carbs. Over the years many a snotty Porsche driver challenging the Fleetwood had gotten a long look at my old-fashioned trunk disappearing into the distance.

I drove slowly around the house and turned up the hill. There were acres of green lawn. The narrow road was lined with giant oaks, and a few hundred yards from the house a small stream bubbled down through a corridor of weeping willows.

The whole horse-racing scene usually leaves me cold. But as I slid beside half a mile of sparkling white fence and saw gawky yet graceful colts trotting along keeping pace with the Fleetwood, the old saw about "improving the breed" suddenly seemed like more than just the collection of words it had always been.

I came to a crest and saw the track spread out before me in a little valley between my hill and the steeper slopes of Blood Mountain.

The sun was just burning off the mists down below. The place was certainly no Churchill Downs. One small grandstand faced me. The wide oval of the track was fenced in with more white pickets. I could see small figures walking horses around the buildings. My narrow lane joined a wider road, which was, I assumed, the main one that would bring patrons when and if the track opened. I drove down it and parked near several other cars in a huge parking lot.

The main entrance was closed up. I walked

round the fence and found an open gate. Inside, with the exception of three young men—boys, really—walking horses, the place seemed deserted.

"Hey," I yelled, "where can I find Loyal Boone?"

One of the boys pointed at a small building alongside the grandstand. I went over and stepped inside, right into the middle of a shouting argument.

Loyal was facing a heavyset man of perhaps fifty who alternated inarticulate curses with threatening movements.

"What the hell do you care?" the man bellowed. "We can all get killed and you won't pay it no mind."

"That's not true and you know it," Loyal said.

The man swore again. I noticed three other men against the wall. They all wore gray work clothes. "Tell that to poor old Jesse Simpson," said the man. "I'm drawing my time before something happens to me." He turned to the others. "You men coming with me?"

"I jest don't know, Clarence," said one of them.

I moved over toward Loyal. The man named Clarence whirled on me.

"You think this one'll help you?" he jeered, pushing his big face right up against mine. He had very bad teeth and they didn't do his breath much good. "This Yankee? Hell, they shot at

him and his woman out on the back road and h[e]
didn't even raise a finger."

"Back off, friend," I said. "I've got no quarre[l]
with you."

"Hoo, boy!" said Clarence to his friends. "Th[e]
Yankee ain't got no quarrel with me. Well," h[e]
said, moving even closer, "I sure got a quarre[l]
with you. This is none of your business, so g[o]
packing."

"Just a damned minute," Loyal began. I qu[i]eted him with a wave of my hand.

"Don't push it too far, Clarence," I said. "Col[o]nel Brown has hired me to find out what's goin[g]
on around here. I can use your help. We won[']
get anywhere fighting among ourselves."

Clarence didn't take the olive branch. Spat[t]ering my face with his angry spit, he made se[v]eral vivid and anatomically impossible sugges[-]
tions.

Then he said, "And the same goes for you[r]
blond hoor."

I don't remember hitting him. During a life[-]
time of scuffling to keep my brains from bein[g]
bashed out, helped along by two intensiv[e]
courses in unarmed combat—one with the U.S[.]
Marines, one at the New York City Polic[e]
Academy—I have been programmed as a[n]
efficient killing machine. As a result, I try t[o]
keep my anger under control. It is patheticall[y]
easy to kill a man with your bare hands if yo[u]
know what to do to him.

Suddenly Clarence was on his hands and knees, gasping and puking. He was lucky. Two inches higher and my fingers would have driven into the massive nerve center of his solar plexus and he would have been dead.

"How about the rest of you?" I asked tightly. "Do you want to dump on the lady the way your idiot friend here did?"

"Not me," said one. "Listen, Loyal, we're not mad at anyone. But Clarence had some good arguments. We sure don't want anything to happen to us like it did to Jesse."

"That's what I'm here for," I said. "We're going to find out what the hell's going on, and who's doing it."

"I sure wish you men'd stay," said Loyal. "We need somebody guarding the track until this mess gets straightened out. I tell you what, we'll put on a few more guys so we've got two men on a shift together. And raise the pay to twelve dollars a day."

The men looked at each other. One nodded almost imperceptibly, and then the rest nodded too.

"All right, Loyal," said one. "You always been fair with us, and so has the Colonel. We'll stick."

They went out, pointedly not looking at Clarence, who was now pulling himself up by the edge of the table.

"Hoo, boy," he said, choking a little. "What'd you hit me with—a two-by-four?"

"I hit you with my fist," I said, still mad. "Would you like to come back for seconds?"

He waved his hand. "Not me, mister. You got a wallop like a kicking mule."

"Get off the track, Clarence," said Loyal. "I'll send your things to you."

"Anything you say, Mr. Boone," Clarence said. He rubbed his stomach. "Mister, I take back the things I said. I had me an awful time with the old woman last night and she said she'd put me out of the house if I didn't draw my time. I was more mad at her than I was at you. I don't usually talk like that about a lady."

"Okay," I said. He stepped toward me and I tensed. But he was holding out his hand. I took it and he squeezed until I thought my knuckles would pop out through the skin like marbles. Then he grinned and loosened the pressure.

"You're all right, Yankee." He went out. Loyal took a newspaper and threw it over the mess Clarence had made.

"I've been thinking," he said as we stepped outside, "things are moving pretty fast. It might be better after all if you had some kind of official status. I've got a friend, Judge Jasper Holland. He's retired, but he's still legally a member of the bench. I think we ought to have a talk with him, see what he can come up with."

"Sounds good to me," I said. "It might be nice to have a little buffer between me and Sheriff

Goff. Like, for instance, if Clarence goes to him with an assault story."

Loyal laughed. "Don't worry about that. Clarence may call you out sometime to try and give back a little piece of what you gave him, but he'd never ring in the Law on a personal fight. I think you may even have shown him the error of his ways. He's not a bad man; he's just got a nagging wife and he hits the corn a little hard."

To my uneducated eye the track looked completed. But Loyal showed me where work still needed to be done.

"That whole track's got to be dragged and combed out a couple more times. Everybody talks about racing on turf, but these days you hardly see it any more."

"What's turf?"

"A grass track. It takes too much upkeep to stay in shape. What we're going to have is a standard dirt track. See those big rollers? We're using them to pack down the hard dirt base. Then we stir up a soft cushion a couple of inches deep to keep the horses from busting their feet."

As we walked down the track, we passed the starting gate.

"Just a hunk of metal," he said gloomily. "Somebody knew what he was doing when he monkeyed with those magnets."

Inside, under the grandstand, he showed me the betting windows.

"What's that?" I asked, pointing at a huge blackboard at one end of the room.

"Something I hope we never have to use," he said. "That's a tote board. It dates back to the eighteen hundreds."

"I thought you used that Totaliser gadget."

"I hope so," he said. "But if we can't lease one, I don't see how the Colonel can come up with a million dollars to buy one."

We wound up back near the parking lot. Loyal looked at his watch. "It's a little after ten. Why don't we drive downtown and have a talk with the judge."

"Fine," I said. "And while we're there, is there any way I can have a few words with Uncle Uglybird?"

"Miz Simpson's yarb doctor? No problem."

As we drove back down past the house, I saw Charity and Subrinea riding alongside us on the other side of the white fence. I gave a wave and they waved back. Charity looked beautiful, her blond hair tossing with the horse's gait.

"We'll be back for lunch!" I yelled.

As we passed the house, Aunt Jenny came out and waved a white towel at us. I waved back. She called something, but I couldn't make out the words.

"Aunt Jenny fixed the coffee this morning," I said. "I think she wants me to come back and finish it."

Loyal grinned. "You'll survive."

106

Gethsemane was white and neat under the morning sun. It was odd to think that a beautiful little town like this could harbor murder and corruption.

I parked outside a small frame house two blocks from the hanging stoplight that marked the center of Gethsemane's main drag. We went up on the porch and Loyal banged on the brass knocker.

"Door's open," called a voice.

Loyal swung it open, motioned me inside. The room within was gloomy and dark. The curtains were drawn against the bright sunlight.

"That you, Loyal?" asked a voice from a dark corner.

"Yes, Judge," said Loyal. "Do you mind if I draw the curtains? Can't see a damned thing in here."

"Draw away," said the judge. "Who's your friend?"

"Ben Shock from New York City," said Loyal. "We asked him down to look into the mess out at the track."

"Heard you had a killing there yesterday," observed the unseen judge as Loyal pulled the heavy curtains away from the window. The light flooded in, and then I saw him for the first time, a wizened man sitting in a huge Morris chair. His gnarled hand was wrapped around a glass of brown liquid that I immediately knew wasn't Doctor Pepper.

"Jesse Simpson," said Loyal. "Burned to death."

"How about a drink?" suggested the judge.

"Not for me," said Loyal. "Too early in the morning."

"Mr. Shock?"

"No sir," I said. "Maybe later."

The judge lifted the glass and sipped from it. "I've just been sitting here, thinking," he said. "I reckon I'm going to die soon, and there's so many things I never learned. It makes a body mad to think on all the things he's missed."

"You didn't miss much, Judge," said Loyal. "My daddy says you went through this county like a locust. It's a wonder there's a pretty woman or a jug of shine left for any of the rest of us."

The judge laughed. His hand trembled as he put down the glass. "Your daddy doesn't do so bad for himself, I hear," he said. "All right, boy, I know you didn't come here to swap stories. What's on your mind?"

Loyal told him. He described the shooting on the back road, Jesse Simpson's death, the copperhead in Adger Brown's bed.

"They're after you all right, Loyal," said the judge. "I don't know who, but they've got you penned in pretty good. What do you want from me?"

"Ben Shock here and his partner are going to be looking around some for the Colonel," said

Loyal. "Ben's already had one run-in with Matt Goff, and depending on how high up our unknown friends are, they might cause him a lot of trouble. Unless we could get him some kind of official standing."

"Why don't you go to your cousin, Tom King? He's the county attorney now."

"He's also a boot-licking, toadying little coward," said Loyal. "I wouldn't trust him as far as I could throw him."

The judge laughed. "Family love and respect, that's what I enjoy seeing. Tell me this, boy—why should I get involved? What do I care if your track gets open or not?"

"You care," said Loyal, "because you care for this county and this state. You know the track will bring money into Buckhorn County. The county and the state will split fifteen percent of the handle on every bet made at Butterfield Downs. That'll come to ten, twelve million dollars a year clear—and just part of that can put this town and this county back on its feet. You know as well as I do that tobacco's almost gone."

The judge sighed. "You're right there, son," he said. "So many things we thought were a lasting part of our lives are gone. The railroad doesn't run, the farming's just about played out. Even the hemp industry's gone. I remember when we used to provide hemp for just about every ocean-going boat in the water. But there hasn't been a hemp license issued since nineteen sixty. Hunting and fishing's gone to pot, too. Now you got to have a season and a license for everything. There's too many people and not enough game. I guess the state's just about wore out for folks like us."

"Not wore out, Judge," said Loyal. "It's changing, and we've got to change with it. It isn't any better or any worse than it used to be—just different. People are going to the cities now instead of the land. They've got to, to make the money. That's why Colonel Brown's track is so important to the county. Would you rather someone came in and set up a factory to make guided missiles?"

"No," said the judge, "you're right. Mr. Shock, what credentials do you have now?"

"None," I said. "Until three weeks ago I was a sergeant on the New York City Police Force. I resigned."

"Ben killed one too many crooks," said Loyal. "Up there they don't like to hurt criminals."

The judge laughed gently. "You sound like my kind of man, Ben. What's your partner's name?"

"Charity Tucker."

"A woman?"

"One of the best you'll ever meet."

"I take your word on that," he said. "Leave it to me, Loyal. I'll call my friends in Louisville, get an authorization for your friends to act as investigative officers of the court, reporting only to me. We'll keep it under cover."

"Thank you sir," I said.

"Thank *you*," said the judge. "If Loyal Boone recommends you, I have no doubts that you will be a credit to this court."

I held out my hand. He ignored it. Stung, I put it in my coat pocket.

"We'll talk to you later, Judge," said Loyal.

We went out. Loyal took one look at my face and laughed.

"Don't get your dander up, Ben," he said. "The judge wasn't insulting you. He just didn't see your hand."

"He'd have to be blind not to," I said, still hot.

"He is," said Loyal. "That's why he stepped down from the bench. Judge Jasper Holland is as blind as a post."

10

Uncle Uglybird McGee was as ugly as they had said and then some. He was also as bald as an egg. His skin was dark ebony, except where a purple scar angled down across one cheek. His teeth, when he grinned, were dark with tobacco stains.

When he spoke, his voice was a surprise. It was low and cultured.

"Shortly after the First World War," he said, "I sailed on a merchant vessel out of New Orleans and jumped ship in Jamaica. I lived in Kingston for nine years, and I fear my orientation is now more British than American."

"So is your accent," I said.

"That's what sets me off from the rest of the yarb doctors in these hills," he said, grinning. "A lot of hill people, especially the younger ones, would secretly rather go to a city doctor. But their ways are against it—and they don't have the money. I am accepted as a compromise between Lexington Hospital and the illiterate faith healers. My record of cures, I might add, is higher than the average—primarily because I supplement my native herbs with a few of the mycins and other antibiotics my medical friends downtown slip me on the QT."

"Uncle Uglybird," I said, "you must have one hell of a sense of humor."

"Son," he said, "I am sixty-seven years old. With a face like this, if I didn't have a sense of humor I would have killed myself fifty years ago."

"We're asking about Jesse Simpson," said Loyal.

Uncle Uglybird shook his head sadly. "You should have seen that poor man before we cleaned him up. He looked like something dragged up from the pits of hell."

"What killed him?" I asked.

"Third-degree burns all over his body. He must have inhaled the flames, too. He died in seconds.

"Chuck Wallace said his clothes weren't even singed," said Loyal. "How could that be?"

Uncle Uglybird spread his hands. "Who knows?" he said. "He could have been dressed after he died. Or, what the hill people are saying could be true."

"What are they saying?" I asked.

"That it was the hand of Satan claiming one of his own. The black magic of the Devil dragging another screaming sinner down into pools of burning brimstone." He scratched his bald head thoughtfully. "That's what killed poor Jesse, you know."

"What?"

"Flaming brimstone."

I felt as if I had walked uninvited into one of those horror TV movies. "You mean like fire and brimstone and all that stuff?"

"Exactly, Mr. Shock," said Uncle Uglybird McGee.

11

When we got back to Butterfield, Aunt Jenny ran out of the house crying.

"Where you-all *been?*" she asked tearfully. "I tried to stop you when you drove by, and now those two girls have had to go up to Lexington all by their lonesome."

"What's happened?" Loyal asked tensely.

"It's the Colonel," sobbed the woman. "Mr. Loyal, he's dead."

"Adger?" said Loyal numbly.

Aunt Jenny nodded. "They called right after breakfast. They said they found him dead this morning."

"What happened?" I asked.

"I don't know, Mr. Ben. Miss Subrinea and Miss Charity drove right up there when I told them."

"How long ago did they leave?" Loyal asked.

"More than an hour."

"Let's go," he said.

As we came down out of the foothills, I really opened up the Fleetwood. Loyal put both feet up against the firewall and said, "Faster." We were going ninety at the time.

When we got into Lexington there was a blinking traffic light. "Turn left here," he said. A few blocks further and we were at the hospital.

The receptionist was flustered by the intensity in Loyal's voice, but she directed us to the second floor, where another receptionist clucked sympathetically and took us to a suite of rooms at the end of the corridor. The first room inside the door was a sitting room with a television set and a portable bar. Beyond it was a bedroom. Subrinea and Charity were in there with a doctor. Subrinea was looking down at a man who lay half-covered by a sheet. The face was aquiline, with a bushy white mustache and a strong mouth set in a frown. Even from the next room I could tell that the man was dead.

Charity looked up and saw us. Loyal started toward the bedroom. Charity came out fast, followed by the doctor, who shut the door.

"Howdy, Mr. Boone," said the doctor.

"I'm going in there," said Loyal.

Charity touched his arm. "Not just yet, Loyal. Let her be alone with him for a little."

"What happened?" I asked.

The doctor sucked at his teeth. He looked embarrassed.

"This is Mr. Shock," said Loyal. "He's working—he was working for the Colonel. Now he's working for me."

"Well," said the doctor, "Colonel Brown appeared fine when the nurse looked in on him last night. But this morning he was dead."

"What time this morning?" I asked.

"Why . . ." The doctor sucked at his teeth again. "Well, we called you folks around ten, so . . ."

"What time did you find him?" I said.

"Nine-thirty," he said reluctantly.

"Why so late? I thought hospitals got everyone up at seven a.m."

He sucked his teeth embarrassedly. "Usually we do, but the second-shift nurse was in the room with him, and no one else thought to disturb the Colonel."

"What was the second-shift nurse doing?" I asked.

"Sleeping," the doctor admitted slowly. "I don't condone it, Mr. Shock. She has already been reprimanded. But she's a good nurse and they're hard to come by. She says she doesn't remember anything except feeling very tired, and then it was nine-thirty and she found that the Colonel had expired."

"Great," I said. "When will you know what killed him?"

"Why, his heart," he said.

"Is that an opinion or a fact?"

"An opinion, sir, but we all know that the Colonel's heart—"

"Loyal," I said, "I want you to get Subrinea to request an immediate autopsy."

"She will," he said. Then, to the doctor, "You heard me. Start getting things ready. She'll authorize it as soon as she comes out of there."

"Very well, Mr. Boone." The doctor sucked his teeth once more and huffed out of the room.

Charity pressed up against me and hugged my neck. "Oh, Ben," she said sadly.

"Where does this leave Butterfield?" I asked Loyal.

"That's up to Subrinea," he said. "She'll inherit everything. If she wants to continue with the track, that's her prerogative."

"Do you think she will?"

"Ben," he said grimly, "I think she'd let herself be torn apart by wild horses before she'd shut down Butterfield now."

When she came out, Subrinea was calm and very precise. Loyal kissed her. She did not respond noticeably. When he suggested the autopsy, she nodded.

"They killed him," she said.

"Now honey, we don't know just what happened," Loyal said.

"They killed him," she repeated. "Ben, I don't give a damn about the track any more. But it's right in the middle of this mess. So I'll open it if it takes every dime my daddy left. Those vultures will be circling around. I want you to find them for me."

"We'll do what we can," I said.

Her hand gripped me so hard that my wrist went white. "Do more than that, Ben. *Find* them. I want them dead."

"Leave that to the Law, pumpkin," said Loyal.

"Goddamn the Law," she said. "This is my daddy they killed. The Law doesn't come into it. This is between me and them."

I understood her. Once again the veils had parted, and this time I was looking back at the pioneers who had sired Subrinea Brown.

"Do you want to stay up here, Subrinea?" Loyal asked.

"No," she said. "Call whoever you have to. Make the arrangements. I'm needed in Gethsemane."

Loyal went over to the telephone and started dialing. Charity put her arms around Subrinea. Over Charity's shoulder, Subrinea's eyes met mine. They were tearless and as cold as two pools of ice water.

"Ben," she whispered, "promise me you'll get them for me."

I promised.

12

A kind of manic purpose had seized Subrinea. She refused to remain in Lexington a moment longer than necessary to sign the required papers for the autopsy. By six that evening, we were back in Gethsemane and the four of us were driving out to the home of Harmon Boone, Loyal's father. Blue huddled in the back seat.

"Harmon's associate director of the track," said Subrinea. "He'll have to take on some more responsibility now."

I remembered Loyal saying that his father had not returned from Mexico until he was already in college. "How did he get involved?" I asked.

"Money," Loyal said shortly. "There's no point in trying to hide it, Ben. My daddy and I don't see eye to eye on a lot of things he did when I was a boy. But sooner or later, especially in a small town like this, you've got to let bygones be bygones. Adger found himself recently in the position of being land poor. He must have been worth ten million dollars, but he couldn't put his hands on enough cash money to option all that Blood Mountain property he needed for the track. My daddy had the money. Adger needed it. A partnership was born."

"You're too hard on Harmon," said Subrinea. "I agree he was a polecat when he was a young man, but he finally came back and tried to make amends."

"That's what it looks like," Loyal agreed. "Too bad it came too late to do me or my Aunt Cecelia any good."

We were well back in the hills by now, driving toward the lower ridge of Blood Mountain.

"Take it easy along here," said Loyal. "You can see the house when we get around that next curve."

A hundred yards ahead the road climbed over the slope of another ridge and disappeared in a gentle curve around the summit.

The sun was low and slanting in from the left when I drove over the top of the hill.

You read about people gasping, but this was the first time I could remember actually hearing someone go "Gasp!"

The someone was Charity, and I had a hard time not echoing her. I touched the brakes and pulled the Fleetwood over to the side of the road so we could look at the view. What we saw was as complete a surprise as if we had suddenly found ourselves on the moon.

The Boone house was more like a small village, nestled in a gentle valley. The sun gilded the rooftops, and far down below I heard a dinner bell clanging.

"It's beautiful," said Charity.

The style of the main house and the smaller ones surrounding it was Mexican. The roofs were red tile, and a thick white wall surrounded everything.

"It ain't much," said Loyal, "but Pappy calls it home."

"Do you live out here, too?" asked Charity.

"I have a room," he said. "And Blue stays out here most of the time. But I mostly live in town."

"Loyal has a dungeon he calls an apartment over his office," said Subrinea. Her voice was light. It would have been impossible for an outsider to know that her father had died this day.

"My stepmamma, Maria, designed this layout," said Loyal. "My daddy says he built it to keep her from feeling lonesome away up here in Kentucky. And of course the Mexican laborers who work the snake farm live here too."

"What snake farm?" I asked.

"One of Daddy's enterprises," Loyal said. "He'll tell you all about it if you give him half a chance. Anyway, I think Mexico ruined Daddy for anything as common as an ordinary house."

He waved a hand at the little village below us. "This lets him feel important, lets him be *el patrón grande.* You can call daddy Don Harmon the First."

I started the car and drove carefully down the winding road. At one particularly sharp curve we passed almost directly above the roof of the main house. One mistake with the wheel and the Boones could easily have had a Fleetwood dropping in through the ceiling.

Close up, the place was even more impressive. A lot of care and money had gone into those buildings. The gate that blocked the road was genuine wrought iron. I half expected Zorro to drop from one of the balconies—mask, cape, and all.

It was a letdown when a Mexican wearing a dirty T-shirt, tattered khaki trousers, and hippie-length hair stepped out of a doorway and presented us with the business end of a double-barreled shotgun.

Loyal leaned out of the car. The Mexican recognized him and opened the gate.

"Guards and everything," said Charity. Her voice was sharp. The magic had been broken.

"Up here in the hills," said Loyal, "law and order becomes a pretty personal thing."

We drove through the gate. The house within was much bigger than it had appeared from the hill. Except for the thick lawn, violent green in the fading light, you could have mistaken this place for an estate in Cuernavaca.

A Mexican woman, fat and cheerful, let us in. Loyal led the way past heavy Colonial furniture into the dark gloom of a study that lay just off the main hall. The lamp shades looked like genuine Tiffany, and the books that lined the walls were bound in leather.

A rather small man wearing a dark blue business suit got up from a reclining chair behind the massive wooden desk. He was anything but swashbuckling—not at all the figure I had expected Harmon Boone to cut. But as he stepped toward us and held his hand out to Charity, it was easy to see that here was a man who did not need external paraphernalia to establish his command. His posture, the set of his bushy white head, the steely look of his eyes—all said that Harmon Boone was a man used to being obeyed.

"Pleased to meet you, ma'am," he said. "It's a real honor to welcome another beautiful woman to these hills."

The happy Mexican woman arrived with an elegant hostess wagon. It was piled with sparkling glasses, a wooden ice bucket, bottles of club soda, and nestled incongruously in the middle of it all, a simple stone jug very similar to the one I had nipped from at Jesse Simpson's sitting-up. Near it was another bottle wrapped in straw.

cating the stone jug. He took up the straw-encased bottle and poured a hefty slug of white liquid into one of the glasses. "As for me, I spent so much time in Mexico that the only thing opens up my throat any more is tequila. We have this made special down in Vera Cruz."

"Mountain dew," Harmon Boone said, indi-

I took mountain dew. Charity opted for the tequila, which she drank neat after sprinkling some salt on the back of her hand. She bit into a lemon and I felt my lips pucker.

"Little lady," said Harmon, "you drink tequila like you've been south of the border."

"I covered the Olympics for TV," she said.

"A newslady?" He raised his bushy white eyebrows.

"Used to be," she said.

Loyal briefed his father about us quickly. "You heard about Jesse Simpson," he said.

"Terrible," said Harmon Boone. "No way at all it could have been an accident?"

"I don't think so," I said. "He was burned to death and stuffed back into his clothes before Butterfield's trainer—Chuck?"

"Chuck Wallace," said Loyal.

"Chuck Wallace was able to get back to the feed room. There wasn't any evidence of fire in the room, and Jesse's overalls weren't even singed."

"I don't see how anyone could dress a man in the time it would take Chuck to get from his

128

his office to the feed room," said Harmon Boone.

"You've been out there?"

"My boy, I am associate director of Butterfield," he said. "I make it a point to check out every aspect of my business. And that includes the distance from Chuck Wallace's office to the feed room."

"I agree with you," said Charity. "I timed how long it took us to walk, not run, the distance. Less than twenty seconds."

"The fact remains," I said, "his clothing wasn't burned, so someone must have dressed him after he died."

"Chuck Wallace?" asked Loyal. "You don't suspect him, do you?"

"I don't suspect anyone. But facts are facts." I turned to Harmon. "I understand you put money into Butterfield. How does that make you associate director?"

He threw back his head and laughed. "Money talks, boy. But that's not the reason. In its infinite wisdom, the state government requires all tracks to have a board of directors made up of responsible citizens to sponsor the operation. That's to keep the syndicate boys out, and prevent any hanky-panky. My investing in Butterfield had nothing to do with my being named associate director. That was due to the great regard the community, and in particular Adger Brown, felt for me."

"That's why we're here," said Subrinea. "My father's dead."

Harmon Boone sat down as suddenly as if he had been struck with a blackjack. He put his glass down heavily, spilling part of the tequila.

"No," he said.

"He died sometime last night up in Lexington," said Subrinea. "We don't know what of, but we will. Meanwhile, I need your help. I am not going to let them keep us from opening the track. Are you willing to take over where Daddy left off?"

"Subrinea," said Harmon, still looking dazed, "I don't know what to say. I knew Adger was feeling poorly, but—I never thought it was this serious."

"It may be more serious than you think, sir," I said. "There's a good possibility that he was murdered."

Harmon made protesting sounds that faded away when his son told him about the copperhead that had been placed in Adger Brown's bed.

"You never told me that," Subrinea said questioningly.

"The Colonel didn't want me to," said Loyal.

"You should have told me," she said.

"My God," said Harmon. He got up and put his arms around Subrinea. "Of course I'll help you, child. I don't take any stock in this murder business, but I know how much that track meant

130

to your daddy. We can't let it go down the drain. It'll be his memorial."

The words were corny, but the emotion with which he said them wasn't. I found myself with two equal—and opposite—reactions to the man. The first was an immediate attraction to him. The second was an instinct not to trust him. He was too good to be true. I have learned through bitter experience as a cop that when you like a man too fast there's always a good chance that he's a con artist working a grift on you. I dug in my mental heels and refused to form an opinion yet about Harmon Boone.

The front door banged opened and I heard voices arguing. A man and a woman stepped into the room and stopped, obviously surprised to see the crowd.

Standing a step ahead of the woman, the man caught my eye first. He was dark and lean, obviously Mexican. He wore the traditional Mexican riding garb of short jacket and tight pants that belled out over elegant hand-tooled boots. Flashing silver spurs were strapped to his feet. His head was shaded with a wide sombrero, and his waist was encircled with a gun belt that suspended matched pearl-handled pistols. The belt's loops were filled with live ammunition. Here in the hills of Kentucky his outfit should have been laughable, but the dark intensity in his face discouraged the impulse to laugh or even smile. His eyes probed one face, then another.

Without a word he turned and left the room.

The woman moved closer to the single lamp with its butterfly shade. There was only one reaction a man could have to a woman like her—an instant, virtually overwhelming urge to rip her skirts up around her neck and bed her right there and then. She projected sexuality with such intensity that I felt the sweat pop out on my forehead. I was afraid to try my voice. I sensed that it would probably croak if I attempted words.

She was obviously Harmon's wife from the way she assumed possession of the room and everyone in it. Her eyes flicked past mine, then returned. I wasn't fooling her. She saw into my face, knew exactly the reaction she had produced. It was something she was used to in men.

I glanced at Charity. Her eyes were like gun slits in a forbidding fortress looking down over some ill-advised vessel caught trying to run the blockade. It's rough having a girl who can read you like a book. Especially when it's a dirty book.

Harmon stood up.

"Miss Tucker, Mr. Shock, my wife Maria y Juana Isabela Mendoza de Boone. Maria, Miss Charity Tucker and Mr. Benjamin Shock."

Maria, now that I looked *at* her instead of just reacting *to* her, was considerably younger than her husband. A dark beauty straight out of a Velasquez painting (she made you think of

132

things like that). She held out her hand. Charity took it as if she had been offered the head of a serpent.

Maria's hand was hot and moist in mine. I dropped it as quickly as I decently could, looking over her shoulder at Charity, who suddenly grinned and stuck out her tongue at me. I grinned back and relaxed. Maria, not missing this byplay, gave me a sly grin of her own.

"You have a beautiful home, Mrs. Boone," said Charity.

Before Maria could answer, Harmon said, "This is an exact replica of the Mendoza house in Mexico."

"Yes," she said. "In fact, my husband had to be restrained from dismantling my father's home and shipping it to Kentucky stone by stone." She turned to Subrinea. "My dear, I was shocked to hear about the accident at the track. I hope it will not cause you further difficulties."

"Maria," Harmon began, "Subrinea . . . "

Subrinea picked it up there. "My father died this morning, Maria. That is what brought us out here. But, much as it may disappoint you, neither what happened to Jesse Simpson nor my father's death is going to slow down the completion of the track. We intend to open on schedule."

"Now, Subrinea . . . " Loyal began unhappily.

Harmon stepped between the two women. "Let's not have any more quarreling over that

133

blamed track," he said. "Maria, Subrinea is under a severe strain this evening and—"

His wife interrupted. "Subrinea, I am distraught to hear about your father. We all loved him. And I am sorry that you and I do not agree about Butterfield Downs. I realize that you are deeply involved in this, particularly since your father was so dedicated to the track. But others may have reasonable grounds for opposing it. I do not go so far as the superstitious Unknown Tongue in believing that the track will corrupt Gethsemane with sin. But I have lived in other primitive places where happiness and joy vanished when modern values and attitudes were enforced on people who were not ready for them. I think what your track will do is destroy the happiness of our town and our people."

Subrinea laughed. *"Your* people?"

"I was born Mexican," said Maria, "but I am American now. I am also Kentuckian. I belong to Gethsemane. It is my town and my people. I have been happy here, and I do not want to see these hills changed. But I admire you, and I am happy for Loyal. I wish we could be friends."

Harmon cleared his throat and stared into his tequila glass. Loyal looked at Subrinea, then at Maria.

Finally, Subrinea said, "Maria, I'm sorry. If

you want someone like me for a friend, you're welcome to me."

Maria hugged her. "Come into the kitchen. We will have coffee."

"I've got to talk to Harmon," Subrinea said.

"There is time for that later," said Maria, leading Subrinea from the room.

"It's about time those two got together for some friendly talk," said Boone.

Loyal scuffed his foot uneasily. "We've got an awful lot to do."

"We'll get to it," said his father. "Meanwhile, what say I show your friends around the snake farm?" He looked at Charity and me. "I reckon it smells a bit gamier than Disneyland, but odds are you'll remember it a lot longer."

Charity gave a little shudder, and I said, "That's kind of you, but as long as we're up here I'd sort of like to see the Unknown Tongue community."

"Easy as pie," said Harmon Boone. "That's where my snake farm's located."

"What kind of snakes do you raise?" asked Charity.

"Rattlers, moccasins, adders."

"Copperheads?" I asked.

"Those too." He got up and gestured toward the door. "Let's get going while the light holds."

"I think I'll stay here with Subrinea," said Loyal.

"Suit yourself. Ben? Miss Charity?"

I gave Charity a glance. She looked unhappy, but she gave a slight nod.

"We're right behind you," I said.

13

I wouldn't have been so quick to follow Harmon Boone if I had known that the only way to get up to the snake farm and the Unknown Tongue community was on horseback.

Over the years, my relationship with horses has not been a pleasant one. I get saddle sores on a merry-go-round. After the age of fourteen, when I rode a docile pony around a half-mile track at Asbury Park, the only physical contact between me and horses was when a mounted cop's nag stepped on my foot during a Columbus Day Parade up Fifth Avenue.

And here I was, ten feet in the air clutching a saddlehorn as a big brute under me waggled his way up a mountain trail. The horse, who knew I was scared, seemed to take a mischievous delight in stepping as close to the edge of the drop-off as his lummox feet would take him.

If I had been last in line, I would have dropped out and hiked back down to the house in the valley. But Harmon and Charity were both behind me, riding their mounts with the loose-gaited ease that comes only with long practice. Ahead of me was the Mexican who had entered Harmon's study with Maria.

He had been introduced to us as Hector Mendoza, Maria's cousin. He bowed deeply to Charity and gave me a limp hand to shake. There was a faint lisp to his voice when he spoke. I gave him the benefit of the doubt and attributed it to Castillian pronounciation. Mendoza sat his horse as if he'd been born in the ornate Spanish saddle.

The trail widened a bit and Harmon drew his mount up alongside mine. I was delighted. He was between me and the drop-off.

Nodding at Mendoza, I said, "If they ever shoot any Zorro movies down this way, there's their leading man."

Harmon's expression made it clear that Mendoza was not one of his favorite people.

"Hector joined us three years ago," he said. "He's plenty smart. Keeps those Mexicans in line. That's why he wears that getup. He looks so much like a *patrón* they snap every time he appears."

"I thought the days of peons and *patróns* were over in Mexico," I said.

138

Harmon laughed. "Nothing ever changes. They brought in land reform and gave the *peones* their own farms, but a hundred men still run the country. And they still ride around on horses with silver saddles and gold coins sewn to their pants legs. Anyway, Hector pretty much runs the snake farm for me. That frees me up for my other operation—real estate, things like Butterfield Downs, and so on."

"What exactly do you do with the snakes?" I asked.

"Extract venom. Sell the critters to zoos and carnivals. There are only two or three snake farms in the country. One's down in Florida, another's in Texas. But I think we've got as efficient a farm as any there is." His jaw tightened. "I got to say, Hector's the one who makes it work."

"How?"

"He runs those hands on a tight rein. Without saying anything against Mexicans, those half-breeds we've got up here will take a mile if you give 'em an inch. Hector can be a mean hombre when he's riled, and those breeds know it. I saw him work over a drunken Mex who came at him with a knife, a big bastard half again his size. He put him down pronto with his fists, and then started working him over with one of those silver spurs. Well, a little bit's fine, but when he started for the throat I had to step in." Harmon spat. "I broke it up all right."

139

"Broke it up?"

"Flattened Hector from behind with a two-by-four." He laughed. "He's family, you know. That seemed better than going at him with my fists. Less personal. Besides, if I had he mighta whupped *me*."

Ahead of us, Mendoza touched his horse with his spurs and the animal quickened to a fast trot. We were well up the side of the mountain now. Harmon pointed toward the crest.

"Over the top and down the other side," he said, "is Butterfield Downs. We're on the north slope of Blood Mountain."

The trail began to narrow. Harmon drew up ahead of me and broke into a trot to follow Mendoza. I held my pace. I was damned if I was going to gallop up any mountain with three hundred feet of eternity falling off to my right.

"Chicken," called Charity.

I made a cock-a-doodle-do sound at her.

We came over a ridge, and through the trees I saw some dingy gray buildings. They were scattered haphazardly around the side of the mountain. The slope was so steep that most of them were perched on stilts that looked to be fifteen or twenty feet tall on the lower end of the buildings.

We rode into the outskirts of the town, if that was what you could call it. The shacks were depressing as hell. The boards were weather-beaten, and I doubted that they had ever seen paint to begin with. The rickety porches were crammed with rocking chairs, hanging swings, galvanized washtubs, and laundry.

Gaunt dogs lazed beside the road. They looked up at us and slunk away, showing their teeth, tails between their scabbed legs. There wasn't a human being in sight.

Then we passed a two-seat outhouse located just a few feet from the road. The door was open. One of the seats was occupied by a bearded, overalled man. He glowered at us as we rode by. Charity, who had pulled up to ride beside me, nodded and said, "Smile, you're on Candid Camera." If the man heard, he didn't react. Neither did I. This was a very unfunny place.

There must have been twenty-five shacks. Although we passed them all without seeing another person, I sensed that we were being watched from within.

Beginning a hundred yards or so beyond the shacks there was a heavy growth of jack pine. We rode through it a few minutes, then suddenly came into a clearing. There, surrounded by the wild hills, a modern cinder-block building, windowless and framed with handsome spruce trees, filled an area roughly the size of a city block.

I whistled. It was like coming across a Howard Johnson's in the middle of the Mayan jungle.

We followed Harmon and Mendoza to a hitching rack and dismounted.

"Some little place you've got here," I said. "How did you get all these cinder blocks up that hill?"

"We didn't," he said. "We poured them here. Come on inside."

The door appeared to be locked. Mendoza made what was obviously a signal with the buzzer. I couldn't hear it, and he blocked my view with his body, so I couldn't get the sequence.

The door opened and we went in. The room inside seemed the size of Madison Square Garden. It was lighted from overhead with fluorescent tubes. Harmon nodded his head toward them. "One in every six is a sun lamp," he said. "The temperature in here is maintained at an exact eighty-three degrees."

"Where do you get the power?"

"A diesel generator out back. Then there's a standby gasoline generator, and backup nickle-cadium storage batteries that could keep the lights and heat going for twenty-four hours."

"That's some investment," I said.

"It pays off. Last year we grossed over half a million from venom sales alone."

"A lot of snakebite kits."

"Most of the venom is used in medicine," he said. "Especially that from the cobra and mamba families."

We walked between row on row of glass-walled cages. They were filled with sand or wood

142

or even water. The only common denominator was snakes. Every cage housed from one to a dozen of them.

I felt the sweat running down my nose.

"Do snakes have to be this hot?" Charity asked.

Harmon shook his head. "No ma'am. But if it drops much below this, they get lazy, won't eat. If they don't eat, they don't grow. And besides the fact that we get paid by the inch when we sell the snakes themselves, a bigger snake gives more venom."

Charity took my arm.

"If the temperature gets down to, oh, fifty or so," said Harmon, "most of these critters go into hibernation."

"What happens if it goes down to freezing?" Charity asked.

"They die."

We were near the center of the huge room now. Surrounded by a waist-high metal wall, like an above-ground swimming pool, was a big sandy pit. In its center, working around a group of small tables, were half a dozen men who were obviously not Mexicans. They were bearded, and wore faded blue overalls and heavy ankle-high shoes.

"Now you see why I built my farm up here," said Harmon.

"Unknown Tongue," I said.

He nodded. "It ain't hard to raise snakes and take care of them. What's hard is milking them for their venom. There aren't a dozen men in this country qualified to do that. Except for these people."

Charity and I watched, fascinated. Silently, without appearing to notice each other, the hill men walked carelessly between clusters of coiled snakes that writhed around on the sand. Every so often one of the men would bend over and hold the palm of his hand toward one of the reptiles.

"Look at that," marveled Harmon. "You ever see anything like that in all your born days? Look at that rattler try to strike at him. But when he holds his hand like that, the critter's snout hits his hand before the fangs do."

I saw what he meant. One of the snakes was trying to take a nip out of an overalled man's hand and getting nowhere fast. It struck, hit the outstretched palm, then found itself caught behind the triangular head.

Charity gasped. "What's he doing now?"

The man had bent over and, still holding the rattler's head, wrapped its body around his arm.

"Those snakes get pretty panicky," said Harmon. "Some of them weigh eight, ten pounds. That's enough to break their fool necks if they don't wrap around something."

Charity looked like she wanted to throw up.

The man went over to one of the tables and picked up a small glass jar. Something white was stretched over its open neck.

"Heavy muslin," said Boone. "Watch. He'll poke that critter's fangs through it."

I watched, and he did. The man began to massage the back of the snake's head with his free hand.

"Squeezing the poison glands," said Boone.

"I hear music," said Charity.

I listened. So did I. A Beethoven string quartet, of all things.

"They must have been turning the tape over when we came in," said Harmon. "The snakes like music. Especially this classical kind. It gentles them down."

"Good for Beethoven," I said.

The man was finished with the snake. He went over to the metal fence, where a Mexican was waiting. The second man took the snake's head carefully, supporting the reptile's body with his other arm, and headed toward a row of glass-walled cages. He slid the snake into one and closed the lid.

"What would happen if that snake bit him?" I asked.

"Not much," said Boone. "The venom's almost all gone. He might get pretty sick, but that's all."

"How about those men?" asked Charity, indicating the hill men in the snake pit.

Harmon shrugged. "Once or twice they been bit. Their buddies hustle them out of here before you know what's going on. They aren't a damned bit scared of those reps, and none of them's ever died or even been laid up from being bitten."

"And they're willing to work for you?" I said.

"Only up here," he said. "I tried to get them to come down to the flatlands, but they turned me down cold. Up here it's tied in some way with their religion. And since they won't have anything to do with the folks down in the valley, this is the only way they can get cash money for stuff they have to buy."

I wandered around to the other side of the pit to get a closer look at the milking process. It was enough to make the hairs on your neck stand up.

An open door led through the far wall into another room. I turned toward it. Suddenly, Mendoza was in my path.

"That is shipping area, señor," he said. "Nothing to see."

Harmon came over, took me by the arm. "I want to show you the prize snake in the whole shebang," he said. "A New Guinea coral snake. The most poisonous critter in the world."

Beyond the open door a telephone rang. Harmon's hand jumped on my arm. "Hector," he said, "that's the phone in the storage room."

"Yes, *patrón*," said Mendoza. He went inside and closed the door.

Mendoza had told me it was a shipping room, and now Harmon was calling it storage.

We went over and looked at the New Guinea coral snake. It was a pretty little thing, about as big around as a pencil and colored with bright red, black, and yellow stripes. It was coiled around a stalk of celery.

"He's cute," said Charity, leaning forward for a closer look.

The snake saw her and opened its mouth and lunged forward. She shrieked and leaped back. I noticed that it had no fangs and mentioned it.

"Nope," said Harmon. "They wait in a tree branch and catch you on the face or neck. They're like a turtle. They just hang on and chew. And the minute they break the skin, you're dead as sure as a bullet'd been put through your head. There's no antivenom made that'll save you in time."

"Why do you have this one, then?" I asked.

"Those heart transplant people use its venom to make antirejection drugs. They water it down a couple of million times and mix it with some other stuff, and it apparently knocks out just enough white blood corpuscles to do the job."

We went outside again. The sky was very red now, and the sun had gone down below the crest of the mountain.

"Phew," said Charity.

"Long as we're up here," Boone said, "there's somebody you most likely want to meet."

"Who's that?" I said absentmindedly.

"Blind Judd."

14

We led the horses back into the Unknown Tongue village. The sun was well down now, and purple shadows were climbing up from the valley to swallow the peaks of Blood Mountain.

Halfway through the village Harmon turned off the main trail, and we followed him downhill for a quarter of a mile to a rude clapboard building larger than the others. There was a crude wooden cross nailed to the peak of the roof. The two doors were open, and inside, a golden glow of lamplight washed over rows of rickety wooden benches.

"Son," said Harmon, "I don't know if this is going to work out or not. But we might as well try."

He went inside. Charity and I followed him.

There was a musty odor, mingled with the

earthy aroma of human sweat, burning kerosene, and what smelled like sassafras. There must have been fifty or sixty men and women in the ramshackle church—now I knew why the village itself had been so empty. Most of the women worked paper fans energetically.

They all looked around as we entered. Some nodded at Harmon, some deliberately ignored him. But all gave Charity and me the insolently impersonal stare you might reserve for a visiting Mongol.

"Who goes there?" demanded a stentorian voice. It belonged to Blind Judd, who was perched behind a pulpit high up in one corner of the church. It was reached by a homemade ladder. He had his own personal kerosene lamp, and when he leaned forward the light came up under his chin and nose and made grotesque shadows that would have done Bela Lugosi proud.

"Harmon Boone. I have friends with me."

"What friends?"

"Friends from another place," said Harmon. "They do not understand your ways, and there may have been trouble because of that. But they are here to help us, and want your friendship."

"What friends?" repeated Blind Judd.

"Mr. Shock and Miss Tucker," said Harmon. "I vouch for them."

"*You* vouch for them?" roared Blind Judd. "By what authority do you speak for others? These

150

are the two who have been brought here to aid the Whore of Babylon! She is an unrepentant sinner, and those who tarry with her must be banished!"

"Banish away," I said loudly, mad. "But keep rifles to yourself."

"The harrowing of hell awaits you!" he bellowed. "Pools of fire and brimstone will claim your bones."

Harmon made a move to stop me, but I pushed past him and stood beneath the pulpit.

"You've got a right to handle your religion any way you want," I called up to him. I turned and said to the gathering, "That goes for you, too. Nobody wants to interfere with that right. But get one thing straight. Anyone who comes gunning my way again with a rifle is liable to get a taste of hell's fire himself." I looked up at the impassive face of the blind man. "That's a warning you ought to take," I said. "A blind man who sends other people out to do his dirty work is just as guilty under the eyes of the law as if he'd handled the gun himself."

"There is only one Law," he announced, "The Law of the Almighty, and that Law says to put sinners away from the saved."

"Come on, Ben," said Charity. "This isn't doing any good."

I went back to our little group. I was steaming mad. The men of the Unknown Tongue had all gotten up silently from their benches and were

151

blocking the double doors with their blue-overalled bodies.

"Flee to the hills, to the valleys, to the sea," called out Blind Judd. "The vengeance of the Lord pursues you and will prevail."

I looked at Harmon, then at the men bunched in front of the doors.

"How about this?" I said in an undertone. "Do we have to fight them?"

"I hope not," he said. "Follow me."

He walked slowly and purposefully toward them. We followed. Near the rear of the church a slim, darkly beautiful girl slipped from her bench and pressed by us. She smelled nicer than the rest. Her body was warm against me for a second, then she was past us and confronting the men.

"Let them pass," she said to the leader. He hesitated, looked over her dark brunette head at us, then gave a slight nod. The ranks parted and we walked between them.

We got on our horses and got the hell out of there, riding down the mountain in the deepening dusk. No one said a word.

15

When I reached in my pocket for the Fleetwood's keys, I found the note. It was a crumpled scrap of paper that looked as if it had once belonged to a paper fan. I remembered the fans in the Unknown Tongue church—and the girl who had brushed against me.

Scrawled penciled words read, "See Brother Randolph."

I looked at Loyal and asked, "Who's Brother Randolph?"

"I told you about him," he said. "He used to be the preacher for the Unknown Tongue, before Blind Judd turned up."

"Is he still around?"

"I think so. I believe he's working on a tobacco farm out near the Lexington turnoff."

"I want to talk with him."

We got back in the car and drove up the curving road, sweeping around over the roof of the Boone estate.

After we'd gotten back from our horseback ride up the mountain, Harmon had quickly agreed to help Subrinea over the next difficult weeks.

"We'll get that track open," he promised. Maria said nothing.

The car was crowded. Harmon and Maria were following us in a neat little Porsche. Blue took up most of my front seat and Loyal, Subrinea, and Charity were in the back.

I applied a little pressure to the gas pedal. Blue looked out the window, gave an uneasy shudder, and lay down on the seat with his paws over his eyes.

"I think I'm going to keep Blue in town a while," said Loyal. "He may not be the bravest dog in the world, but he can howl just about the loudest. I had a hunch a couple of days back that maybe somebody was poking around my office. I don't think we ought to take any chances right now."

When Harmon had invited us to have dinner with them, I assumed it was to be at the Boone home. But here we were on our way back to Gethsemane to visit a restaurant called Aunt Sue's.

As we topped the crest of the ridge and started downhill toward the town, Loyal said, "Aunt Sue lived in Mexico for ten years after her husband died. Then she came home. Except for some of the workers up at the snake farm, she's the only one in these parts who knows how to make a good bowl of chili."

"I'd have thought your stepmother would have a cook," I said.

"She does. He's French and he cooks everything in wine."

We stopped at Loyal's office. He opened the door and gave his dog a friendly tap in the ribs with his toe. "Get in there, Blue," he said. "Keep an eye on things for us."

Blue gave us a sad hound dog's sigh and loped inside. Loyal locked the door. He sighed himself. "Never thought I'd see the day when you had to lock a door in Gethsemane," he said.

We left the car in a grove of oaks a quarter mile from town and climbed upon a huge front porch. The Porsche was already parked nearby. We heard mariachi music coming from an open window. Aunt Sue had obviously brought more back from Mexico than a chili recipe.

Loyal led us in without knocking. Inside, we entered a large room that held six or seven tables. It was dim with candlelight. The mariachi music was coming from a huge juke box at one end of the room. It seemed incongruous.

Harmon and Maria were already seated at one table. We joined them. With six, it was crowded.

A buxom woman arrived. She had long blond

hair and looked about as Mexican as Shelley Winters.

"Put yourself in my hands," she boomed in a deep contralto. "We may not be fancy, but I promise you the best food this side of Mexico City. Margaritas to start off?"

There wasn't any point in fighting City Hall. We ordered Margaritas. While we were waiting for them, I looked around the room. Over in one corner, almost hidden by the jukebox, Mayor Oppie Hornbuckle and Sheriff Matthew Goff were huddled over two bottles of beer. I nudged Charity and she took in the view.

We toasted with the Margaritas. The salt burned my lip, but I managed to swallow some of the concoction. I have never understood why people take good liquor and louse it up with lime juice and such.

Aunt Sue reappeared with a platter heaped with what looked like green mush.

"Guacamole," Charity said knowingly, reaching for a frito. She scooped up some of the green stuff, dumped a red sauce over it, and munched it happily. I tried the same and almost choked to death. Whatever Aunt Sue put in her red sauce had to include at least fifty percent cayenne pepper.

Maria was even more unlucky than I had been. She broke her frito in half with the first bite and dumped a couple of tablespoons of gunk all over her dress.

She dabbed at it with a napkin, then excused herself and left the table.

"I'm sure glad you two straightened out your problems," Harmon said when his wife was out of earshot.

"So am I," said Subrinea. "It's just that it seemed as if everyone was ganging up on my father about the track."

"She believes what she believes," said Harmon. "But she wants you and Loyal to be happy."

"You met her in Mexico?" asked Charity.

Harmon nodded. "I'd made my pile and had already booked my train ticket back to the States." He grinned at me. "Private car, I might add. Then I met Maria, and that cost me another two years. I had to woo her, win her, and then persuade her to come to Kentucky. You don't do that in a month."

The tension was easing all around. We had another drink and started talking about the uniqueness of Harmon's snake farm.

"I was raised as an Unknown Tongue," he said. "Back then they started the boys handling snakes at the age of eight. Girls started at ten."

"You?" Charity said incredulously.

Harmon shrugged. "You can't choose which way to be born," he said. "But all that ended when my mama and papa got caught in a freak tornado before they could get to the storm cellar. I ended up in an orphanage run by a hardshell Baptist, and that pretty well decided me against any religion at all. Well, I grew up, got married, and had me a son. Loyal here. His mama was a pretty little thing, and we were doing right well. Then she got pregnant again and caught the childbed fever and died. That took the heart out of me. I just couldn't stay around here any more. I left Loyal with his aunt and took off. I didn't know where I was going, and I didn't care. I bummed around for a while, and then I ended up in Mexico.

"Things worked out pretty good for me down there. That was where I made my pile, up in the mountains mining silver. I was just about ready to come home when I met Maria. She was out riding and her horse shied and threw her, then run off. She was trying to walk back to civilization when she got bit on the leg by a rattler. When I found her she was half dead and it took all I knew to save her. So all that Unknown Tongue training wasn't wasted after all."

"And that's how you ended up in the antivenom business?" Charity said.

He grinned. "Call if by its right name, Miss Charity. I raise snakes. The antivenom part is the most respectable, but I sell an awful lot of those reps to carnivals and zoos. It's a specialized kind of farming, and there's good money in it."

Hornbuckle and Goff, at the table behind the jukebox, got up and left, nodding at us as they passed.

"Wonder what that bunch is up to," said Loyal.

"Nothing good," said his father. "That's the only thing I can't abide in these small towns—the local politics."

"Do you think those politics can keep the track from opening?" I asked.

Harmon shook his head. "They may make it rough on us, but we can beat them. Leave it to me."

Maria returned. "Have you ordered?" she asked.

Her husband laughed. "We've just been drinking ourselves silly. What would you like to eat?"

"Is there a menu?" Charity asked.

"Sure," said Harmon. "It's in Aunt Sue's head." He called, and the blond woman came out. "This pretty girl would like to know the menu."

Aunt Sue beamed at us. "You're lucky tonight. I had a shipment of fresh turtle meat from a trapper down on Rough Creek. So how does tortuga teriyaki sound?"

"It sounds Japanese," said my girl.

Aunt Sue nodded. "You're right. You take turtle meat, saute it in soy sauce, and—"

We never got the complete recipe. Just then the pay telephone on the wall rang and Aunt Sue answered it. She listened for a minute, let out a gasp, and called out, "Loyal! Your office is on fire!"

We left in a hurry. Harmon and Maria stayed behind to settle up and I kicked the Fleetwood and made it downtown in less than two minutes. There was a crowd gathered outside the white building.

One of the men came up to Loyal. "It's out," he said. "It was just a little one."

White smoke still drifted out the open door. "What happened?" asked Loyal. The man looked away.

There's a little warning that goes off inside my head at odd times. It was clanging like a four-alarm fire bell now. I headed for the door. Loyal beat me to it.

As he went in, he called, "Blue? Blue?"

I smelled an acrid, sulphur-like odor, and with it the sickly-sweet stench of cooked flesh.

"Oh my God!" said Loyal, looking down behind his desk. He bent over and put his hand to his mouth. Just then Charity came in, followed by Subrinea, Maria, and Harmon. I grabbed the women and shoved them outside. Behind me I heard Harmon cursing as he joined his son.

I didn't go back in. I had seen all too clearly what was behind the desk.

Crusted in brown and yellow residue, legs stretched out in final agony, Loyal's dog Blue lay burned to death. And from the overwhelming odor of sulphur in the air, I was willing to bet that the murderous agent had once again been brimstone.

160

16

When we got back to Butterfield, there was a message for me to call Judge Jasper Holland. I looked up the number and dialed while Subrinea made some coffee. Aunt Jenny looked on, sitting quietly in one corner of the big kitchen. Her fingers worked nervously against her apron. All of the life seemed to have gone out of her.

I recognized Judge Holland's voice. "Mr. Shock? Those authorizations came through. You and Miss Tucker are special agents of the court. You report only to me."

I thanked him. He said something that sounded like "Pushtush," and added, "You're trying to help Buckhorn County, so I want to help you. But I better warn you, this appointment isn't going to stay secret more than a few hours. Things have a way of leaking out of Louisville."

I renewed my thanks and hung up.

Subrinea handed me a cup of coffee. It was her own, the good kind. I drank it gratefully.

Loyal sat at the kitchen table. He stared off into the distance. Charity sat near him, speaking to him quietly. He didn't seem to be listening.

"Was anything missing?" she asked.

He shook his head numbly after the question took nearly a minute to sink in. "No. Not that I could see. The safe wasn't touched."

I had a brainstorm. "How about those papers about the track?"

"The option papers? I don't remember. It doesn't matter anyway; those are only copies. The originals are on file in the courthouse."

"What if they aren't?" Charity had leaned forward sharply to ask the question.

"What?" said Loyal, not really listening.

"I said, what if the option papers aren't on file anymore at the courthouse?"

He shook his head. "I don't know what you mean."

"I mean," she said, "that if your copies were destroyed or stolen and someone had lifted the originals out of the courthouse, what proof would you have of the whole land deal?"

He absorbed that for a while. Then, "Mr.

Mulhulland still has his copies. He wouldn't have any reason to renege on the deal. That land isn't worth a damned thing except to us."

"Where is he?"

Loyal shrugged. "Nassau, I think. He doesn't live around here any more. Why?"

Charity looked at me. "Ben," she said, "I think we ought to find out about those papers."

I agreed. "Loyal, you've had enough for one night. Let me have your key."

"You wouldn't need it," he said. "They broke the door down to get at the fire."

"Okay," I said. "I'll drive down and look for those papers. Where would they be?"

"Green file cabinet," he murmured. "In a folder marked Mulhulland."

I finished my coffee, gave Charity a quick peck on the cheek, and fired up the Fleetwood. The night was clear and a burst of stars stared benignly down at me. That's one thing you forget in the city, the incredible size of the heavens. Maybe that's one reason for the things that are wrong with us. Although, to give the cities their just due it's been a while since New York has had a rash of brimstone murders.

The sulphurous odor still choked the office. I opened all the windows. It didn't help much. A strolling band of crickets set up shop outside and serenaded me as I rummaged through Loyal's files.

163

There was a folder marked Mulhulland in the third drawer of the green cabinet. It was empty.

I went through all the other files too. It took over an hour. There was no trace of the option papers.

I went upstairs and looked through Loyal's private apartment. He lived simply. The furniture was old and well used. His private desk was locked, but the super-key I always carry opened it easily. The only thing of interest there was a marriage license issued to Loyal Boone and Subrinea Brown. It was dated six weeks ago.

I put it back, turned off the light, and padded down the stairs. As I was looking around the office to see if I had forgotten anything, I realized that I had—and it wasn't a very pleasant thought.

The back yard was dark. I struck a match and felt my way among the bushes.

Under the elm tree I found the fresh earth. The shovel was still there, leaning against the tree. I blew out the match and let my eyes adjust to the darkness. With the moon just rising, I could barely make out what I was doing—but I managed to reopen the tiny grave. It wasn't that deep. When my shovel struck the burlap bag, I probed more carefuly, and then I had to dig with my hands. The acrid odor of sulphur filled my nostrils.

Blue was heavy, but I managed to lift him out.

The dirt pattered down into the shallow hole like rain.

I piled my stiff, malodorous burden in the trunk of the Fleetwood alongside the skin diving gear I always carry back there. My car was going to stink for a month, but it couldn't be helped.

It took me twenty minutes of doubling back and forth on dirt roads to find Uncle Uglybird's rude cabin. At first, the building looked dark, but then I saw a candle's flame in one back window.

"Uncle Uglybird?"

A shadow passed in front of the candle and a voice said, "Yes? Don't I recognize your voice?"

"Ben Shock," I said.

"Of course," came the rich Jamaican accent. "Come in."

"Maybe you'd better come out," I said. I told him about Loyal's dog. He swore. "It's bad enough for people to fight amongst themselves," he said, "But a man who'd kill a dog isn't fit to live."

He helped me lift the burlap bag with its horrible contents out onto the back porch.

"I'll look him over as soon as it's daylight," he promised. "But I can tell you now, it was brimstone."

"That's what I think too," I said.

"What about Mr. Loyal?"

"He seemed all right," I said.

"Don't let what he looks like fool you," said Uncle Uglybird. "He loved that hound. I vow he's busted up inside."

I promised to keep an eye on Loyal and left. Halfway back to Butterfield I remembered I had left the hole open behind Loyal's office. I cursed, but there was nothing else to do but go there and fill it in again. It would be unnecessarily cruel to let him discover someone had stolen Blue's body.

Subrinea and Charity were still in the kitchen, having graduated from coffee to Scotch. Aunt Jenny was gone, and so was Loyal.

"He's upstairs, sleeping," Subrinea said. "He put down around eight fingers of white lightning and just caved in." She finished her own drink. "Which," she went on, "is what I am just about ready to do myself." She gave Charity a friendly hug, kissed my cheek and said good night.

"Alone at last," said my girl.

When I told her what I hadn't found in Loyal's office, her eyes narrowed. "That might be it," she said. "A land grab of some kind."

"We'll know tomorrow when the courthouse opens," I said. "If those papers aren't on file there, we'll know the whole thing had nothing to do with the track at all, but with the land Adger Brown wanted to buy."

"The Lexington Hospital called," she said. "There's some kind of hangup on the autopsy. They want to run more checks."

166

I nodded. "That doesn't surprise me. That whole deal smelled funny." I poured myself a slug of Scotch. It went down like honey after some of the things I'd been drinking lately. "Listen, baby," I said, "I've got some legwork to do tomorrow. I've got an idea about prying open our friend Sheriff Goff's shell. So why don't you check out the option papers."

"Done," she said. "Also, I've got calls out to some of my broadcast buddies at CBS in Louisville. I want to check up a little deeper on some of the principals in this mess."

"Do that," I said. "And don't get mad, but you shouldn't overlook Subrinea."

"I won't and I wouldn't," she said. She leaned forward and kissed me, and for a moment I was able to forget about the burned, twisted body of the poor dog named Blue.

17

For all the sleep I got, I might as well have stayed up and stared at the stars. The ceiling kept falling on me, and every time I was on the verge of sleep, the bed dropped out from under me suddenly and I came awake with that breathtaking start that makes you reach for the light switch and a cigarette.

Judge Holland's warning that our assignment as agents of the court would probably not remain secret very long had given me an idea.

I dropped Charity at the courthouse and parked the Fleetwood outside the combination jail and sheriff's office.

Goff was surprised to see me. He offered me a paper cup of coffee. I declined. Aunt Jenny's efforts that morning had turned me against the brew permanently. I told him I wanted to make a statement.

He made a phone call, asked someone to come over. Then he looked up at me and said, "We don't have any police stenographer. We'll use the public girl who operates over at the library. All right?"

"I couldn't care less."

We stared at each other for five minutes, and then a spectacled woman in her late fifties scurried in, a steno notebook clutched in one hand. She perched over us on a wooden chair near Goff's desk like a harpy with black muslin wings. Goff didn't bother to introduce us.

"Interrogation," he began, "of material witness, address unknown, regarding alleged shooting on the back road."

"Take this down, too," I said. "Voluntary statement made by Benjamin Lincoln Shock, resident of New York City, regarding attack made upon him and Miss Charity Tucker by person or persons unknown."

"It's just a formality," he said.

"I like mine better."

The harpy looked at him. "Shall I take down what he said?" she asked.

Goff sighed. "Yeah," he said. "Let's keep this moving, all right?" He gave the date, and then asked, "Do you have any idea why a person or persons unknown would want to shoot at you?"

"A pretty good idea," I said. "You see, you

don't know this, Sheriff, but Miss Tucker and I have been appointed special agents of the court regarding alleged harassment on the part of public officials toward the new racetrack."

"Hold on!" he yelled.

"Shall I write—" began the stenographer.

"Hell no," he said. "Don't you write down a damned thing until I tell you." He turned back to me. "What do you mean, you're special agents of the court?"

"Just that," I said. "If you don't believe me, check with Judge Holland."

"Nobody told me about that."

"Sorry," I said.

"That's all," he told the stenographer.

"But—"

He reached over and tore the page from her book. "It was all a mistake," he said. "Put in your bill. I'll okay it."

She gave me a snippy look that blamed me for her lank hair and flat chest and huffed out.

When the door closed, Goff said, "How come you're working for the court? I thought the Brown girl brought you two down."

"She did," I said. "But Loyal Boone thought we needed a little heft. So he prevailed on the judge."

Goff sucked on his teeth. "That boy gets out of line sometimes. When he was County Attorney . . ." He stopped, looked out the window. "I guess that's all, Mr. Shock," he said. "I don't know what's going on here, but it looks to me like you don't need this office."

"Simmer down." I sat on the edge of his desk. "I never thought much of this racetrack deal to begin with. The money isn't that good, and I am allergic to being shot at."

"What are you getting at?"

"I know about the option papers," I said. It was a shot in the dark that connected.

"What option papers?" His voice was far away, as if it had lost touch with his body.

"Don't waste time, Goff," I said. "Do you want me with you or against you?"

"I don't care where—"

"The hell you don't! Now get him over here. Now! Be careful what you say. We can make a deal, but if you louse it up you'll be sorry. I think you know that."

He gulped, but he picked up the telephone and dialed. I clapped my hand over the mouthpiece. "Don't say a word that anyone can understand, especially no names. You know the operator's listening in. Just get him here and your troubles will be over."

"Hello," he said when I removed my hand. "This is Goff. Can you come over, right now? It's important. . . . No, no—not on the phone. . . . Good, see you then."

He hung up. Sweat was glistening on his forehead.

"So far, so good," I told him.

He got up shakily and swung open a file drawer, took out an unlabeled bottle and swigged deeply from it. He didn't offer me any, for which I was grateful.

"Who would have guessed about the judge?" he said. "Somebody's goin' to have to take care of him."

"Goff," I said softly, "anyone who goes near that blind man will have to answer to me personally."

"I thought you were willin' to throw in with us."

"Under certain circumstances," I said.

The telephone rang. My mouth went dry. This might be my pigeon, deciding the deal smelled.

"Got him cold?" said Goff. "Well, hell, boy, you know what to do. Get fifty from him in cash and let him go. If he draws back, tell him the judge is out of town and he'll have to spend the night in the lockup."

He hung up. "Stupid bastards," he said to no one in particular. "You have to teach them how to shake down a speeder. Where do they come from?"

I knew where they came from. On the Force in New York we had started getting them during the past few years. They came from families that hadn't been crippled by the poverty of the Depression, from families that had enough to eat, and who could maintain their pride in never having stood in line for food handouts from Uncle Sam. Goff and I came from another generation; we looked at things with a different eye. It had turned him mean and dishonest. I wasn't sure what it had done to me.

The door opened and Mayor Oppie Hornbuckle barged in. He stopped, looking at me in a mixture of amazement and anger.

"He come over and offered—" Goff began.

"Shut up!" shouted the Mayor.

"Hell," Goff persisted, "he's on the make. He—"

"You idiot!" said Hornbuckle. "Don't you see? He tricked you into bringing me here."

Goff turned toward me, bewilderment on his face. I smiled at him.

"That's just about what I figured the deal was," I said. "If you remember, I never said *who* you were going to bring over. You're the one who called the Mayor."

"You sonofabitch!" said Goff, coming around the desk toward me. He pulled a flat billy from his hip pocket. The way he tapped it against his free hand indicated he knew exactly how to use it. I ignored Queensberry rules and gave him a fast kick between the legs.

He shrieked and fell down.

I stepped backward fast. Hornbuckle didn't seem to represent any danger, but you never know. I didn't have to worry about him. He was so horrified at what I had just done that he was almost as white as poor Goff himself.

"I don't know just how I'll use this information," I told Hornbuckle, "but when the sheriff stops swimming around the room, remind him that if he has any ideas of an assault charge, he might try remembering everything he told me about your little deal. And if he has any trouble, I'll be glad to repeat it all in court."

"Listen, Shock . . ." groaned Goff.

"Don't make it any worse than it is," Hornbuckle said.

The Mayor seemed to have good sense. But I couldn't resist turning the knife.

"My friend," I said, "it can't *be* any worse than it is. He told me everything."

Hornbuckle gaped at me. I walked out. The air was fresh and full of sunshine. It was refreshing after the stench of fear I had just left.

18

You can always tell when a town has gone bad. People gather in little groups, talking in low voices. Their postures are taut and awkward. They have the look of those who have been brushed by brutality and do not know how to cope with it—a look of shame, as if they had somehow caused the violence that frightens them.

Gethsemane was like that as I walked across the town square toward Loyal's office. It was impossible to meet anyone's eye. Whenever I looked at someone, he shifted his gaze somewhere else. It was spooky, but not at all new to me.

We are all, in a sense, innocent bystanders. Oh, there are always a few prime movers, the activators, the energizers who put the forces of the world into motion. But most of us only observe these gentlemen and do not participate in their decisions. Then, when life comes up and kicks us in the rear, we react with surprise and that same embarrassment that I noticed now in the good citizens of Gethsemane.

There was still the smell of burning death in Loyal's office. The books on the walls had a different look, as if they were somehow participants in the flaming disaster that had occurred last night. They looked smoky and smelled of sulphur and charred dreams.

He had obviously gone through his files. Stacks of folders were piled on the desk in front of him. I noticed the empty Mulhulland folder on top of the stack.

He looked up dully. "Hello, Ben."

"You seem busy."

He shook his head. "No. I've just been sitting here for an hour." He looked at the pencil in his hand. "I can't seem to concentrate. I don't understand it. After all, Blue was only another dog. I've had dogs killed before. Run over, drowned, snakebit."

"This was a warning," I said. "That's the crunch. You don't know who they're after—you, your father, or Subrinea. It's natural it would shake you."

He put the pencil down on the waxed wood of the desk and contemplated it.

"Ben," he said finally, "I want Subrinea to give up the idea of the track."

"She won't."

"She has to. And I want you and Charity to go off the case."

"Nope," I said. "Sorry, but that wasn't the deal. We go all the way. If you want to quit paying us, that's your business. But the job doesn't stop until it reaches an end."

He put his head in both hands. After a while he said, "All right, Ben. I'll talk to her. And you'll get paid. But I don't feel good about it any more."

"Where does this Brother Randolph hang out?" I asked. "You said he works on a tobacco farm."

"Chester Thurmond's place, out near the Lexington turnoff."

"That's where I'll be," I told him.

Leaving Gethsemane behind me was almost like getting out of jail. I felt free and less under pressure than I had for the past two days. I had a twinge of guilt about Charity, still back there rummaging through the courthouse records. Maybe I'd take her to Uncle Jeff's for catfish and hush puppies tonight.

Thurmond's place was easy to find. I drove alongside nearly a mile of white fence and then came to a cutoff that had a big sign reading "Thurmond—No. 17." Somewhere else in these rambling hills were sixteen more farms owned by Mr. Chester Thurmond. I placed a private bet that when I met Mr. Thurmond he would not be standing around in pale blue overalls with the knees worn out, sucking on a straw.

I parked just inside the front gate by a complex of buildings. Outside them forklift trucks lugged wooden pallets heaped high with tobacco leaves hung on racks.

As I got out of the Fleetwood, a heavy man in khakis came over, carrying a clipboard. He was obviously keeping track of the comings and goings of the forklifts.

"Help you, mister?"

I'd heard the term redneck. My khaki-clad friend was a red*nose*. His beezer was sunburned to a flaming, peeling crimson. My own nose twitched in sympathy.

"I'm looking for Brother Randolph," I said. It sounded funny. You just don't show up on a farm asking for a Brother anybody.

I was oversensitive. "Sure," said the man with the flaming nose. "He's here."

"Can I see him?"

"Why not?"

I followed him back toward one of the buildings.

"Don't think," he said, "that I usually ring the bell on folks working here. I mean, the past is the past, know what I mean? A man hires out, does his job, that's all I ask and all I'm interested

180

in. But Brother Randolph—well, he's something else. It's plain as day he never did nothing in his whole life that he couldn't stand up and tell a judge, or even his Maker." We reached a corridor between the buildings. "You go down that way, past these warehouses, and out into the field until you come to a section marked G. You'll find him under the tent over one of the tobacco rows."

"Thanks."

"Don't mention it," he said.

As I started away, he called, "Tell him Abner says he'll see him tonight at services. Abner, that's me."

When I found Section G, I saw what Abner meant by tent. Supported on poles about eight feet high was a light muslin covering that sheltered rows of growing tobacco plants from the hot sun.

The tobacco looked like those elephant-ear plants you see in hotel lobbies. Several men were tending them. Somehow I knew which one was Brother Randolph and went directly to him. His back was turned to me as he bent over his hoe.

"Brother Randolph," I said. It came out as a statement.

He turned, and the hackles rose on the back of my neck. His face, his soft beard, the gentle light in his eyes—all made him look exactly like pictures and statues I'd seen of Christ.

"Yes, I'm Brother Randolph," he said in a soft

voice. There was a deep power to his words, like a mountain whispering. "Who's it my pleasure to be meeting?"

"Ben Shock," I said. "Abner told me you were back here. He said he'd see you at services tonight."

"Good," he said. "There's been illness in his home. We were afraid he wouldn't be to able to attend."

"What services are they?"

He spread his hands. "Most of the men in these fields come from far away," he said. "They have no family here, no friends outside the farm, no church membership. In my small way, I try to bring God to these fields."

"Then you're still preaching?"

"Still?" His eyes searched mine. "You know about my past?"

I told him about the girl in the Unknown Tongue church and the note she had slipped into my pocket.

"That was Blind Judd's daughter," he said. "Miss Mary."

"Why would she send me to you?"

"I do not know."

"How did Blind Judd take your congregation away from you?"

"It was the will of God," he said.

"How did God make His will known?"

"We were holding Easter services," he said slowly, turning back to his work. The hoe sliced weeds away from the bases of the tobacco plants as he talked. "We were singing 'My Saviour's Gone To Glory' when the doors busted open and there he stood, Blind Judd. He looked like the fallen angel, railing and hollering, thundering his defiance at the fates and at the Lord himself. He said the Good Lord had sent him to the Unknown Tongue to protect the people against the workings of the Devil. That hit home. You see, we'd been having a spell of bad death tokens— owl hoots at midnight, dogs howling on the ridge. Folks were pretty scared.

"Well, Blind Judd said we was all under the Devil's curse for the evil ways we'd fallen into. He pointed at me and said I was the Devil's instrument, that I had led them astray. He told them to drive me out and give him the pulpit if they wanted to be saved from the harrowing of hell."

He worked in silence for a moment. I remembered Blind Judd threatening me with that same harrowing.

"Your people didn't buy that raving, did they?" I asked.

"Not at first," he said. "They looked at me and their eyes were troubled. But they didn't say anything. I made a speech of my own. I told them the tokens didn't mean anything, and even if they did that Blind Judd didn't have fitifying powers to make them go away. I asked him who he was, where he had come from. He didn't answer. He just shouted, 'Heed the word of the Lord's messenger,' and stormed out."

Brother Randolph looked down and paused a long moment. "Next day—it was a nice one, clear and sunshiny—Luke Anders' young'un, Chad . . . we found him . . . " His voice was so low I could hardly hear it. "Poor little feller, he was only six. We found him in the back of the church. Covered head to foot with burns from fire and brimstone. His clothes wasn't even scorched. That was the harrowing of hell Blind Judd had warned us about." He stopped.

"I've seen it myself," I said.

"The people went out of their minds," he said. "They came to my place, Luke Anders leading them. They said little Chad's blood was on my hands. They called me the Devil's minion." He touched a scar on his forehead. "Then they stoned me and beat me. They shoved me down the mountain trail. Luke Anders wanted to kill me there and then, but they stopped him. They told me if I ever came up in the hills again they'd stone me until I was dead. They didn't even let me take my Bible."

"How does Harmon Boone's snake farm fit into this?"

"He built it that next year," said Brother Randolph. "Harmon was an Unknown Tongue when he was a boy, and besides, the people don't ever get down to the flatlands any more since Blind Judd started preaching to them. Mr.

184

Boone's snake farm lets them make a few dollars they couldn't get no other way."

"How does Blind Judd keep them under control?"

"Since he come, there haven't been none of those death tokens. He said he was in the middle of purifying Buckhorn County. Then Colonel Brown made plans to open his racetrack, and Blind Judd said that it was evil, that it would destroy the Unknown Tongue and the flatlanders alike. He cut our people off even more completely from the rest of the world."

"Why would his daughter send me to you?"

I had asked that before, and once again he said, "I do not know." He looked up from his hoe. "Mr. Shock," he said, "I'd be proud if you wanted to stay for my services."

"I wish I could," I said. "But I've got to get back to Gethsemane. Another time."

We shook hands, said goodbye. Then he said, "If you should meet Miss Mary again, I'd mightily appreciate it if you could ask her if she knows what become of my Bible."

"I'll do that," I said and left.

"Did you find him?" asked Abner, at the gate.

"Yes," I said, "I found him."

19

Charity was nowhere to be found in the courthouse, so I went down past the jail to what passed for Gethsemane's main street and started prowling around.

I went into a jukebox-blasted frame building that had a sign outside reading "Mike's Bar & Grill." Maybe the jar of Polish sausages behind the bar counted for the grill. There was no other evidence of food around.

Sometimes you have to deliberately play it stupid. I had an uneasy feeling that all of the information we'd gotten so far on this case had come in through a single funnel: either the Boones or someone they introduced us to. It was time for me to widen my circle of acquaintances.

I ordered a bottle of Blatz and sampled one of the Polish sausages. It was surprisingly good—

hot and tangy from the vinegar solution in the jar.

Three other men sat in the room—one at the bar, the other two playing gin rummy at a table. The bartender made a fourth. I addressed myself to him.

"Anybody here know Jesse Simpson?" I asked.

"Who wants to know?"

"Nobody in particular," I said, sliding a five across the counter. "Let's say Mr. Abraham Lincoln."

He didn't touch it. "You already paid for your order, mister."

I heard the door close. The two card players had made their exit.

"Gettin' ready to close, Phil," said the bartender. The beer drinker at the bar looked surprised, but he got up and hurried out without even finishing the brew in front of him.

The bartender went over and locked the door from the inside.

"You better come along with me," he said.

I picked up the five and followed him into the back room.

The two card players were waiting. They grabbed me from behind and twisted my arms up to keep me from struggling.

"Don't break them," I said.

The bartender had already found my shoulder holster. He put the pistol on a stack of beer cartons. Patting my legs, he came across the Philippine fighting knife tucked into my stretch sox.

He flipped the blade open. "This thing sharp?" he asked.

"You could shave with it," I said.

"Put his hand up there," he ordered.

My left hand was wrenched onto the top of a Pabst case.

"Mister," said the bartender, "if you don't see your way clear to telling me the truth about what you're doing in this town, you ain't going to have no thumb left to hitchhike your way back to where you come from."

"Mike," I said, "if that's your name, I'll go you one better. I'll see that thumb and raise you a forefinger."

I stretched out my forefinger and put it next to my thumb.

The bartender hesitated.

"Go ahead," said one of the men. "He's asking for it."

"He won't," I said. "Mike, I've met men who would cut my throat just for practice, and men who'd never cut anything more serious than a pound of pork chops. You're a pork chop man. So why don't we knock off this crap and see if we can do each other some good."

Mike hesitated, then closed the knife.

"Let him go," he said.

The other two did. I picked up my pistol and

put it back in the holster. Silently he handed me the knife.

"I'm working for Subrinea Brown," I said. "I think all the trouble at the track, then Jesse Simpson's death, and now Adger Brown's are all tied in together. I'm not trying to do anything more ominous than get to the truth."

"Jesse said he was worried about something he found up on the new property above the track," said Mike. "He was in here the night before he got killed, talking about it."

"What did he say?"

"Only that he'd found something funny, and that he had to talk to the Colonel about it as soon as the Colonel got out of the hospital.

"Nothing else?"

"Not a thing, mister. That's the God's truth."

"What do you think?" I asked. "Did someone murder Jesse? Or was it what Blind Judd says, the wrath of God?"

The bartender was shaken by the question. After a while, he said, "Mister, I just don't know. I never believed in death tokens before, but what those hill people are saying about the track got a bunch of us to wondering and worrying. I just couldn't say."

"Thanks," I said. This time he accepted the portrait of Abraham Lincoln.

I went back to the courthouse. Still no Charity, so I drove out to check Uncle Uglybird.

There was a fresh mound of earth in the back yard. Neither one of us looked at it.

"Brimstone," he said.

"There never was much doubt," I said.

"You know," he said, "Blue, without wanting to be disrespectful to the dead, never was much of a dog. But he was a loud one. I can't see him letting anyone do what they did without setting up a ruckus."

"You mean burning him with brimstone?"

"No, " he said. "I mean, wiring up his legs so he couldn't kick. And rigging some sort of muzzle so he couldn't howl."

"You're sure?"

He nodded. "The marks were still there."

I told him about the Unknown Tongue child. His eyes widened. "I never heard about that," he said. "They made a real secret out of it."

"Do you think it's the harrowing of hell?"

"Mr. Shock," said Uncle Uglybird, "I think some of the things us so-called men do to each other would have the Devil green with envy. If there's any hell around here, it's the hell we make for ourselves."

I thanked him and drove back out to Butterfield. Aunt Jenny rushed out and said, "Mr. Ben, where have you *been?* Miss Charity's been calling for the whole livelong afternoon." She gave me a number written on a piece of brown paper bag. I dialed.

"Hello?" I said. "Charity?"

"Oh, Ben!" she said. "Where the hell have you been?"

"Doing some homework," I said. "Where are you?"

"I'm in that gas station on the back road. Ben, please, come and get me."

"I'll be right there," I said. "Why don't you have a Dr. Pepper with Lommie Wingbright while you wait?"

"Don't make fun of me," she said. "The place is closed."

"Then how did you get in?"

"Dammit, don't ask so many questions."

"Okay, baby, I'll be right out."

"Ben, wait!" she cried. "Don't hang up!"

"What now?"

"Bring some clothes. Bring me a blouse and some slacks and a bra and—"

"Wait a minute," I said, "are you drunk?"

"I wish I were," she said. "Be sure you come alone, Ben. Because except for a pair of cavalry boots and a blacksnake whip, your partner Charity is as naked as a jaybird."

20

Lommie Wingbright's gas station looked deserted as I drove up. I parked near the gas pumps. They were locked. So was the front door. A sign read "Closed" without any further explanation.

I went around to the ladies' room and tapped on the door.

"Ben?"

"I sell old clothes," I said. The door opened a crack and I pushed the small suitcase inside. The door slammed. I went out and sat in the Fleetwood. In a short time Charity appeared around the edge of the gas station.

She hadn't been joking. She carried a pair of floppy black cavalry boots and a coiled whip. She wore the clothes I had packed.

Sliding in beside me, she said, "Let's get the

hell out of here. Our friend may wise up and decide to look in this direction."

"What friend is that?" I asked, putting the Fleetwood in gear.

She pointed to a small white house halfway up the mountain.

"That," she said, "is the Castle Hornbuckle."

"Hornbuckle as in Mayor?"

"The one and only," she said. Then she shivered. "Oh, Ben, he really is . . . My God, I thought all that Kraft-Ebing stuff was a big fat joke when I studied it. But they really *do* make genuine—dingalings."

"You sound shook, baby," I said. "Why don't you hold it until we get home?"

"All the way up there? I'll never make it, Ben. I've got to tell you what I found. And if I don't have a drink, my nerve ends are going to come busting out through my skin."

"I know just the place," I said. I made the turn around the courthouse square and parked in front of Mike's place.

Charity gave the courthouse a frightened look. "If he's back in his office, he might see the car."

"Good," I told her. "It'd do my heart good to belt a genuine dingaling in the chops."

She clutched my arm. "Damn," she said halfway across the sidewalk. "I forgot the boots." She dashed back and got the ridiculous cavalry boots out of the car.

194

Mike was surprised to see me, but friendly.

"Why didn't you tell me you knew Uncle Uglybird?" he asked.

"I didn't know it would matter," I said. "Somehow I had the idea that it didn't do a Yankee image much good around here to be friendly with a black man."

"Yeah, but he's Uncle Uglybird," Mike said, as if that explained everything. Maybe it did.

We passed up the Blatz in favor of two double Wild Turkeys, and Charity told me her story.

The original of the option deal was indeed missing from the courthouse records. In fact, most of the official records regarding building permits and licenses were either missing or covered with nitpicking violations that made it easy to see why the track construction was running months behind.

The more Charity searched, the madder she had got. Finally, she decided to interrogate our friend Mayor Oppie Hornbuckle.

"*Interrogate?*" I yelped. "Who the hell do you think you are, Perry Mason?"

"Shhh," she said, and continued.

The Mayor was missing from his office. His secretary, accepting Charity's outdated press credentials as valid, volunteered that the Mayor had been called to an important meeting, and that he would probably go directly home from there. Home, it turned out, was the white house she had shown me high up on the mountain.

Since Gethsemane had no taxis, Charity promoted one of the police officers to drive her up the hill. Let in by a housekeeper who was just preparing to go downtown for some shopping, she produced her outdated press card again and managed to bring off a story about interviewing the Mayor for a TV appearance.

"The Mayor won't be home for an hour," the housekeeper told her.

"I don't mind waiting," Charity said.

The housekeeper went through a mental process of biting her fingernails before she decided that Charity could be trusted. She admitted her to the Mayor's library.

No sooner was the woman's car out of sight than my girl started prowling.

It was more of an office than a library. In one corner a squat Thermofax copying machine sat on a table. An electric typewriter was on a wheeled table.

Most of the desk's contents were innocuous. One drawer was locked. It opened to Charity's master key set.

A square packet of Polaroid photographs brought her eyes wide open.

They were similar in pose and subject matter. In each one, the leading character was Mayor Oppie Hornbuckle. In a grotesque way they reminded Charity of the naked-baby-on-the-rug shot that all proud parents seem to take. But in this case the naked baby was Oppie Hornbuckle.

There was a second participant in each photograph—a nude woman wearing cavalry boots and holding a whip.

The women varied from picture to picture. Some were even black. Most covered their faces with masks.

Feeling sick, she put the pictures back in the drawer.

"Fascinating, aren't they, Miss Tucker?" said a voice. It was the Mayor, standing in the door. He came inside. "Entering under false pretenses. Breaking open my desk. I think a five-year burglary charge would stand up."

Frightened, Charity made a desperate effort. If Hornbuckle's tastes ran to boots and whips, there was a good chance that he would be responsive to the kind of dialogue that she hesitated to repeat even to me.

She burst into the coarsest, toughest speech she had ever heard, let alone spoken herself. She threatened him with castration, promised, "If you get me sent up, when I get out I'll find you, tie you up, and whip you within an inch of your miserable life!"

To Oppie Hornbuckle this was love talk. He forgot who she was and what he had caught her doing.

"You're a good-looking woman," he said. "It would be a shame to send you to prison. That food would make you fat and ugly in a year."

She told him foully and graphically what do do with his food.

He smiled nervously. "There's another way." he said.

She piled on the abuse. He loved it.

He went to a cabinet and took out a pair of high cavalry boots, a whip, a Polaroid camera, and a small tripod.

"Put these on," he said. "You'll be the loveliest girl in my collection."

Charity almost lost her nerve then. But she managed to snatch the boots from him and give him another blast of profanity. His eyes were glistening as he unbuttoned his shirt.

"I'll change in the bathroom," she said desperately.

"Not a chance," he grinned. His hand caught her blouse and a button snapped off.

"Hold on, buster!" she yelled, giving him another series of insults. Then, slowly, she undressed.

As she cast about wildly for some way out of the predicament, he fumbled with the camera.

"Damn it!" he said. "No film."

He gathered up her clothing. "Put on those boots," he said. She did. He handed her the blacksnake whip. She had a wild impulse to strike him with it, but resisted.

"I'll be right back, little lady," he said. "I've got film upstairs." He tucked the bundle of her clothes under his arm. "I don't think you'll be going anywhere until I get back," he said. At the door he turned and added, "You just be patient, honey. I'll show you a good time."

"He made two mistakes," Charity said. "He left my purse. And he didn't think I'd walk out of a house stark naked in the middle of the afternoon. I grabbed a handful of his dirty pictures in case we needed them to stall off that burglary charge through a little blackmail of our own. And I hightailed it down the hill, clutching that damned whip as if it were *protection*, hiding behind bushes and in a dry stream bed until I got to the highway. Getting across the road was a little scary, and I don't know what I was going to tell Lommie if he was inside the gas station. But it was closed, so I busted the window and used the pay phone to call you. End of tale."

I bought her another drink. Then I wiped the nervous grin off her face.

"You crazy broad!" I said. "Where were you when they passed out brains, behind the door? When you roped me into this fool partnership of yours it was theoretically assumed that you possessed the intelligence God gave a newt. Don't you know the risk you took going up there like that? And what the hell do you think would have happened if that frigging camera had been loaded?"

"But it wasn't," she said in a little girl's voice.

"No, it wasn't," I agreed. "For which we both should thank whatever benign Deity that watches over stupid dames. Listen, what do you think I would have done if he—if you . . ."

I didn't have to say the rest of it. I couldn't have if I had tried.

"You're right, Ben," she said in her chastened, tiny voice. "But the Polaroids weren't the only thing I got out of the Mayor's desk." She fished down inside one of the boots and came up with half a dozen photos. I glanced at the top one. They were exactly what she had described to me. And Oppie Hornbuckle was not my idea of sexy art.

She dug around in the toe of the boot and fished out a crumpled yellow piece of paper. It was a Thermofax copy of what appeared to be a map.

"What's this?" I asked.

"I found a map under Oppie's art collection," she said, "I had just long enough to make a copy of it and slip it back before I cleared out."

"Why the hell did you do that?"

"I didn't want him to know it was missing. Look at it, Ben."

The copy was a bad one. Faint, almost unreadable. But readable enough. It was a U.S. Coast and Geodetic Survey map. I found the town of Gethsemane down in the right-hand-bottom corner. The roads and buildings indicated on the map triangulated the rest of the area for me. I found Butterfield Downs and, up the mountain from it, the optioned land that Loyal had described to me.

There was a complex of buildings drawn in on the map, right in the middle of the land in question. I looked at this part carefully. There was no doubt: this was the area that Subrinea's father had taken options to buy.

But the building complex drawn in there had nothing at all to do with racetracks. Instead, written in neat letters was the notation "Site for proposed public nuclear power development." And under that, rubber-stamped—CONFI-DENTIAL.

21

There was a strange car parked behind the Brown home. As Charity and I got out of the Fleetwood I knew somehow that our dinner date at Uncle Jeff's would never come off.

Inside, a heavy, shaggy-haired man was talking with Aunt Jenny. He wore delicate granny glasses. At his feet was a doctor's bag.

"Aunt Jenny," said Charity, "who's sick?"

The shaggy man turned and contemplated Charity gravely for a few seconds. When he spoke his voice was deep and gentle.

"The one who is sick, my dear," he said, "is I."

Charity gave him a double-take. Aunt Jenny went "tcch-tchhh," in a way that indicated she was all too familiar with the shaggy stranger's ways.

"This yere is Doctor Appleyard," she told us.

"Miss Subrinea took to feeling somewhat poorly early on, but she's brighter now." She beamed on Dr. Appleyard with obvious affection.

Appleyard pushed his glasses higher on his nose with one finger. Promptly they slid down again. He spoke as if Aunt Jenny had not interrupted him.

"And the reason I am sick, my dear"—then, nodding at me—"and sir, is that it destroys my soul to see a lovely, spirited young woman like Subrinea exhibiting less good sense than God gave the humble jackass. She seems determined to assassinate her good health by assiduously avoiding proper food, rest, and relaxation."

"Subrinea's had a bad couple of days," I said.

"I know," he said. "Perhaps a bad couple of decades would be more like it. Long walks. Quiet days. Contemplation. Those are the specifics for long life."

"Shoo, that's so," said Aunt Jenny. "The Doctor, he means that Miss Subrinea ain't been takin' proper care of herself for a long time. So he gave her some medicine to give her some soft rest. Later on, I'm goin' to call Uncle Uglybird and get him to bring a yarb tonic. We'll have that poor baby back on her feet quicker than you can say—penicillin."

Doctor Appleyard drew himself up stiffly and raised his hand. "A yarb tonic?" he growled. "For one of my patients? Aunt Jenny, you disappoint me. Have you no proper respect for the pharmaceutical miracles of modern medicine? I shall forget that I ever heard you mention yarb tonic in my presence." He lifted the raised hand to his mouth and whispered to her in melodramatic, back-of-the-hand fashion, "And when you see Uncle Uglybird, tell him Doc Appleyard says, 'Hey,' and if he'll come over tonight I've got some more penicillin salve for him."

Aunt Jenny quivered all over with silent laughter and went into the pantry. I looked at Charity.

"Better close your mouth, baby," I said, "before a passing horsefly roosts in it." I turned to the big shaggy man and introduced myself, then Charity. "What's the story?" I asked. "Will she be all right?"

"When she wakes up," he said. "I gave her enough sedative to keep her out for six or eight hours. Then she'll need some TLC, which I presume will be provided by Loyal. He's up there now, sitting with her." He picked up his black bag. "Well," he said, "Farmer Stone's prize mare is foaling. I'd better get over and hold the patient's head." He nodded at us and left.

"A doll," said Charity, looking after him. "A regular living doll."

I agreed.

Doctor Appleyard was wrong about the length of time his potion would keep Subrinea out. By eight that evening we were all gathering in the sprawling living room.

Historians can talk all they want to about the great inventions and scientific discoveries that have changed history and made life easier for the multitudes. They can discuss the wheel, fire, radium, the Salk vaccine, and permanent voter registration and I will nod sagely and agree that these advances improved the world. But that is mere politeness. For my money, the top genius of them all is the guy who invented the cocktail hour.

The four of us—Subrinea and Loyal, Charity and I—entered that living room wound up like four automatic gyroscopes. But after we belted down a few and talked a while, the tension eased a little. Charity gave me a semaphoric wiggle of the eyebrows that said, "Okay, Shock, turn on the laugh medicine," so I did my Lone Ranger and Tonto joke and then went into a glorious rendition of the blue version of "The Shooting of Dan McGrew."

"Oh, Ben," said Subrinea, "you're a nut."

"Which brings me to my next routine," I said. "Do you think you're up to listening to a progress report on what we've turned up?"

"Not now, Ben," said Loyal.

"No," said Subrinea. "Time's running out. I want to hear what you know."

She poured herself another slug of fifteen-year-old Scotch and sat down.

I rinsed my own throat and began.

"You'll have to bear with me for a little speech

on classic police philosophy," I said. "If you understand a few points on the way cops think, you'll be better equipped to evaluate the facts and working premises we've come up with."

"Get to it," said Loyal. Subrinea touched his arm.

"We're talking about murder," I said. "That's a hard, ugly word." I looked at Subrinea to see how she was taking it. She was hanging in there fine. "Murder doesn't exist in a vacuum. When murder's your business, as it was mine, you learn fast that no matter where the murder occurs—in New York, in New Caledonia, or in Gethsemane, Kentucky—the motives are always limited. To three categories, in fact—the three Ms. Malice. Money. Madness. Maybe they're mixed up—one from column A and two from Column B. But those are the three headings you'll find ninety-five percent of murders under."

"How does that rule apply here?" asked Loyal. "What connection could there be between Jesse Simpson and Blue?"

"Don't forget my daddy," said Subrinea.

"We don't know he was murdered," Loyal said.

"The hell we don't," she said quietly. She nipped at her drink.

"There isn't any sense to it," Loyal said. "No sense at all."

"That's where we come out too," said Charity. "Consider the death instruments."

"Charity means the brimstone and the copperhead," I said. "Of course, the snake failed, but it was *intended* as a weapon. Both of these methods indicate a quality of madness. Whoever thought up stuff like this has to have a badly tilted mind."

Loyal threw ice cubes into his glass with a near violent splash. "From where I sit," he said, "that points to just one man. Blind Judd. He's crazy enough to burn people alive and whistle 'Dixie' while he's doing it."

Subrinea made a little whimpering sound, and Loyal looked embarrassed. He put his arm around her. I chewed at the inside of my lip, glowering into my drink.

When Subrinea settled down, I said, "I'm with you, Loyal. All the signs point to Blind Judd as being a first-rank nut. But we can't lock our thinking in on him because of that."

"He would have needed someone to help," Subrinea said. "After all, he's blind."

"Maybe," I said. "Maybe there were people helping him, and maybe he was even taking orders from someone higher up. Or, and this is a real possibility, he may not even be involved. Consider: If you wanted to commit a murder and there was a wild man in the bushes running around ranting about fire and brimstone and the harrowing of hell—well, what would be slicker than killing your victims in a way that points the finger straight at the nut?"

"But why?" Subrinea asked.

Charity said, "The why, or at least the probable why, is the easy part."

Loyal frowned. "My guess," he said, "is that it has something to do with those land option papers missing from my files. I'd say the tract, or maybe even the whole parcel of land, is the why. Although it's possible that there's madness mixed up in it, too. Madness and a hell of a lot of money, that's my guess."

"Plus maybe some malice," I said. "A triple header."

Subrinea shook her head. "I can't buy that," she said. "Sure, Daddy was a feisty character. But he never did anybody a deliberate hurt in his life. Who would want such a vengeance?" She shuddered. "A copperhead in his bed!"

"Ben said *maybe* some malice," Charity said.

Aunt Jenny came in. "How you feelin' now, Miss Subrinea?" she asked. "Up to some of my fried chicken? If you ain't, I can just push it on the back of the stove."

"No, Aunt Jenny," said Subrinea. "When do you want us to come in?"

"Ten minutes all right?"

Subrinea nodded and Aunt Jenny went away. The scene seemed right out of Kafka. Sweet young thing, sterling guy, both have the hots to get married and make pretty little babies for Grandpappy to bounce on his knee. So what happens? Somebody bumps off Grandpappy. And now, instead of making babies, the young lovers are sitting with a tough ex-cop planning to dig the crazy son-of-a-bitch killer out of the bushes and bust his ass. Bad. I chewed on my lip some more.

"Okay," I said. "Here's where we are. Your daddy took an option on a tract of land. No one objected. He began the construction of a racetrack. No one objected. Then, suddenly, *everyone's* objecting. Public officials are throwing up obstacles.

"Someone puts a copperhead in your daddy's bed. He gets away from the snake, but it brings on a heart attack. He's out of action.

"You take over and bring us in. The ante's been upped. So now Jesse Simpson is found dead. He's burnt to a crisp with brimstone, but his clothes are untouched. Supernatural causes? Or somebody too smart for his own good?

"Next, Loyal's dog Blue is killed. Why? Why kill a speechless dog? Maybe for two reasons. One, to demoralize you. Two, maybe someone had to kill him to get at your copies of the land agreement." I finished my drink, handed the empty glass to Charity. She built me another one, which I really did not need. I went on. "Okay, those are the events. But what do they add up to?"

Loyal spread his hands slowly.

"Well, for starters," I said, "let's not assume that the various events are necessarily connected. We'll investigate each one as a separate phenomenon. Is that smart?"

"No," said Charity. "There has to be a link between them. The legal obstructions to the track. The thefts, the sabotage of the starting gate. The killings, the shooting at us. And what I found . . ."

"But why?" asked Subrinea. "What's so important about the track?"

I grinned at Charity. "Sweetheart, you're on," I told her.

She took out the Thermofaxed map. "I was looking through the desk of our friend the Mayor," she said. She did not, I noticed, mention the state of her attire while doing so. "I found this. It's a map of the optioned land. There's a construction site indicated." She read, " 'Site for proposed public nuclear power development.' "

A tingalingy sound came from the doorway. Aunt Jenny was there, shaking a tiny dinner bell. "Supper on the table," she announced.

"You girls go on ahead," Loyal said. "I want to have a word with Ben."

Charity gave me a quzzical look, but joined Subrinea and left the room. When they were gone, Loyal said, "I hear you met Doc Appleyard before." I nodded, and he continued, "Doc heard from Lexington. They'll have the postmortem results in the morning. And we—someone—can pick up Adger's body then." He looked down at his big hands, Spread loosely on his knees. "Doc says Subrinea's too close to the edge to go through that. I could go, but I hate to leave her. I was wondering . . . "

"Say no more," I told him. "Charity and I have business in Lexington anyway. We'll be glad to bring the Colonel home."

22

There is an interlocking network of personal friendships, referrals, exchanged favors, and general nosiness between the police departments of various U.S. cities that would put Interpol to shame. That night I called my former boss, Captain Murphy of the New York Police Department, and asked him to give me a good referral to the police chief of Lexington. He said he would and I knew it was as good as done.

So when Charity and I arrived in Lexington the next morning, I was ready to do some work. We parked outside the low police building; and while I was chewing the fat with Chief Harlon Caldwell, Charity put her telephone credit card to work and began making some long-distance calls.

Caldwell was both cordial and helpful.

"Buckhorn County is out of our area," he said. "But seeing as how we're neighbors, we keep tabs on a few folks down there."

"What about Blind Judd?"

"Nothing to lock him up on. But he's got a record all across the state for causing mischief. Even been in a rest home once. I figure one day to read his name in the newspaper."

"Ever have anything hooking him up to arson?"

"Arson? Nope, nothing like that.'

"What about Senator Treffit?"

"That's a touchy one, son. After all, the man's a state senator."

"I won't quote you."

"There are those who have hinted that the Senator's pockets are lined with more than lint. No proof, mind you. But his personal holdings are a little fancy for a poor boy who come out of the Cumberland Gap with nothing but a flannel shirt and a pair of overalls wore through the knees."

"But nothing definite?"

"Nope."

"How about Mayor Hornbuckle?"

"Nothing legal. Had a few complaints about the way he likes to get his kicks. No formal action taken, though."

"Sheriff Goff?"

"We ran a check on him once—two, three years ago. He seemed to be spreading too much cash around in the gambling joints over at E-town. He didn't come up clean, but he didn't come up dirty either. Nothing to hang an arrest on."

I sighed. "They're all too neat," I said. "You'd expect at least a traffic violation."

Chief Caldwell grinned. "Not necessarily, son," he said. "Down here we take care of our own. Now I don't mean we'd look the other way if one of those men was really in the wrong. But as long as there ain't no evidence, and with reasonable effort we can't find none, nobody's going to harass them. Especially their own law in their own county. Like I said, any investigation my men've done has only been because Buckhorn's our neighbor and we don't want any rotten apples rolling out of their barrel into ours."

"How about the Boones? Harmon or Loyal?"

"Heard Harmon got into some trouble down in Mexico—but it never got blue-sheeted our way, so that's just hearsay. As for the boy, he's clean as a hound's tooth. Made a damned good county attorney, I hear. Never dug into the till, looked out for folks the best he could."

"Great," I said. "Well, thank you, Chief. I'm back where I started."

"Not quite," he said. "You and me, we may be working together for a while yet."

"How's that?"

"So far all these alleged crimes you've been

talking about happened outside my jurisdiction. But now I've got a hand in the game."

"The Colonel?"

He nodded. "We got the lab report first thing this morning. Adger Brown didn't die from no heart attack. He had enough copperhead poison in his veins to kill a dozen men."

23

We followed the black hearse down the two-lane highway to Gethesemane.

"I didn't get much," said Charity. "The nuke plant's a big secret—in these parts, at least. I had to walk around it to keep from leaking the truth in case my friends didn't know about it, but I dropped plenty of hints. They didn't pick them up."

"Figures," I said. "Probably only half a dozen people in Louisville are on the inside."

"Treffit?"

I shrugged. "Maybe," I said. "But maybe not. Our buddy the Mayor may be the one with the inside track. After all, he had the map. And he had every opportunity to louse up the land option papers."

The hearse turned up the road into Butterfield. We followed.

"Meanwhile," she went on, "the Colonel was in a cash squeeze, all right. I talked to Australia. He was trying to buy one of their Totalisators, but he didn't have the million dollars."

"Who does? Isn't there some kind of credit?"

"If there was, he didn't have it. Maybe because of the sabotage and the harassment."

"They really had him boxed in," I said.

We had telephoned ahead to let Subrinea and Loyal know what time we would be returning. Aunt Jenny had answered the phone.

"They went downtown, Mr. Ben," she said. "They said they wouldn't be long, but they been gone since ten-thirty."

It was now late afternoon. The sun was hot. The wind wafted dusty smells of dry leaves and distant persimmons through the open windows of the Fleetwood.

At a wide place in the road we got in front of the hearse so we could beat it up to the house. There Aunt Jenny, Subrinea, and Loyal were waiting for us. I parked on the grass and we got out.

"Congratulate us," Subrinea said, her voice high-pitched and strained. "I'm Mrs. Loyal Boone."

Charity hugged her. Loyal stood in the shade of the porch, looking uneasy. I didn't blame him. This was one hell of a time to be getting married.

Subrinea came over and hugged my neck. I had thought at first that she was hysterical. But as she kissed my cheek and let her eyes meet mine, I saw it was something else. There was a hard, determined set to her face. Whatever she was doing, she knew exactly what she had in mind.

"All the best," I said.

"Daddy would have approved," she said. "I don't care what people think. Daddy would have been the first to say yes."

Just then the hearse arrived. The driver and his helper got out. I felt Subrinea's hands bite into my shoulders. I turned to look. Her eyes were squinched closed, so tightly that the tears were squeezed out like little clear drops of oil.

"Oh, Ben," she whispered, *"Shut my daddy's eyes!"*

Charity pulled her away, making the comforting whispers that women use at such moments. At the door Subrinea looked at me, perfectly sure of what she was saying. "Please, Ben?"

The hearse driver looked embarrassed. "Sometimes the womenfolk get upset," he said.

"Sometimes with good reason," I said. "Let's take a look before we go inside."

Loyal came over. "Ben, I don't think that's necessary . . ."

"Congratulations on your marriage," I said. 'Maybe she should have asked you. But she didn't. So I'm going to look."

He didn't make any further protest. The driver slid the coffin out onto a rolling platform and opened the top third of the lid.

The mortician had neglected to close Adger Brown's eyelids.

They were wide, staring open.

I heard Loyal suck in his breath. I reached in my pocket and took out two quarters. I put them, heads up, on the old man's eyelids.

"Mister, I'm sorry," said the driver.

I didn't say anything. There wasn't anything to say.

Loyal and I helped the two men lug the coffin inside. In a little room on the main hallway we set it up on two waiting trestles. Aunt Jenny, tears streaming down her cheeks, moved around arranging flowers and draping black bunting over the windows.

I went upstairs and washed my hands. They were hot and sweaty and seemed to smell of death.

In my room I broke out my private stock of Jack Daniels and knocked back two quick slugs straight out of the bottle.

"Save some for me," said Charity. I jumped. I hadn't heard the door open.

There weren't any glasses in the room, so she went the bottle route too.

"I don't recognize her," she said later as we both lay, fully clothed, on my bed. She felt warm and soft in my arms. "She's not the girl I went to school with."

"A lot's happened to her since you traded boyfriends," I said.

"I know," Charity said softly, snuggling up against me. "Ben, what's going to happen?"

"Why ask me?"

"Because I'm all at sea."

"I thought you were the great detective lady."

"I thought so too. But now I'm taking real comfort from knowing that whatever comes up, you'll be here, close."

"I could get closer."

She gave me a gentle slap on the cheek and a soft laugh. We lay silently for a moment. Then I got up and lit a cigarette.

Charity stretched like a big sleekly furred cat. "Mmmm," she said. "I could sleep for a week."

"Go ahead," I said. "I'm going to take a walk. I've got something nibbling around inside my head and it won't come out."

She craned her neck. "Can I help?"

"Uh-uh. Get some rest. Something tells me this is going to be a long night."

She yawned and settled back. I threw half of the light bedspread over her, got a mumbled "Bless you," and went downstairs. The house seemed empty. I looked inside the little room. The coffin lid was closed. At the head and foot of the improvised bier, clusters of long white candles burned.

I took a deep breath and went outside. It was the blue hour. The sun had gone, and twilight flowed, tidelike, over the rolling hills.

My feet crunched on the gravel of the drive. I jammed both hands into my pockets and walked down toward the main highway. A gang of crows—a murder of noisy crows— sat on the fence and cawed at me. I remembered two cartoon crows, Heckle and Jeckle, and wondered why they had been so funny while these real feathered creatures seemed ominous and threatening.

The sky lowered. Black, oppressive clouds sat on Blood Mountain.

Was it money? Malice? Madness?

The nuclear power plant site said money.

The burning brimstone said madness.

The needless death of the dog said malice.

I found myself wishing I could live up to Charity's billing. It would have been very nice to flex my muscles, pluck the offending villain out of the underbrush with thumb and forefinger, and hand him neatly over to the sheriff.

Of course, maybe the sheriff *was* the villain.

Shock, why the hell did you ever come to Kentucky? Why didn't you stay on your little lake, dodging the water-skiers, fishing for the elusive granddaddy of all trout and sipping your beer like the lazy slob you really are?

What does it matter if you bring this particular bastard to book? The woods are full of bastards, and another one will only step forward to take his place.

Sweet reason. No arguing with that conclusion. But somebody has to keep chopping the bastards down. Otherwise, before we know it, we'll all be up to our asses in bastards.

My father was a cop. He made fewer arrests than any cop I ever knew. And his beat was the cleanest, safest, most racketfree beat in New York City. Pop didn't let the punk kids get away with so much that they finally found themselves up on an auto theft rap or a mugging assault-and-battery. He applied the tip of his nightstick where it would do the most good—and while there may have been some sore behinds for a while, there were fewer squeal sheets and criminal records to dog the kids for life.

I wondered what the Supreme Court would have thought of Pop. Not much, I suppose.

The crickets started chirping in the bushes. That's what you're up to, Shock. Keeping the Republic safe for crickets. Or something.

I sighed. Charity had been right. This was the kind of evening to sink into the mattress and forget everything in the brief oblivion of sleep.

As I was walking back up to the house, the cars began to arrive.

24

"Come in, Mr. Ben," said Aunt Jenny. "Miss Subrinea, she's in there."

I followed her gesturing hand and saw Subrinea Brown sitting in the corner of the dining room, surrounded by country women. She was dressed all in black, and her face was half-masked by a veil.

They were all sewing on a crazy quilt. The women's voices were humming a tuneless melody.

"Menfolk's back in the kitchen with they whiskey," said Aunt Jenny.

I looked toward Subrinea again. She did not catch my eye, so I went back into the kitchen.

"Hey, boy," said a voice, and a hand slapped a stone jug into mine. I gave it a swig and handed it back to Jake Morgan, the man I'd met outside

Jesse Simpson's sittin'-up. His brother, Ezra, came over and pumped my free hand.

"Uncle Uglybird spoke up for you," said Ezra. "You all right, mister."

I choked over the white lightning. "Good stuff," I wheezed. It sounded like a replay of the other night.

Loyal came over. He was half drunk. He punched my shoulder and said, "Do you know what she wants to do, Ben?"

"Who?"

"Subrinea."

"No. What?"

"She's scheduled a memorial race this Saturday for Adger. She's bound and determined to open that damned track. I found out because she phoned downtown and had notices put up all over Gethsemane." He fumbled in his pocket and took out a mimeographed sheet of paper. It read, "Pre-season Memorial Race in honor of Colonel Adger Brown. Saturday, 1:30 P.M. All horsemen invited to enter mounts. Public admitted free. This race *will* be run."

"She's some girl, Loyal."

"I won't permit it."

"How can you stop her?"

"She's my wife, remember."

"True," I said. "But the last I heard, Kentucky wasn't observing the Napoleonic Code. The track belongs to her, Loyal, not to you.'

"You're right," he said, swigging from the

stone jug. "But dammit, it's too dangerous for her. She ought to let it lie until we find out who's behind all this killing.'

"I agree," I said. "But don't ask *me* to try to persuade her."

He shook his head and wandered off to talk with one of the Morgan boys. I went back into the dining room and stood near Subrinea until she noticed me.

"Hello, Ben," she said.

"Hello, Subrinea."

"I saw another death token a while ago," she said. "Aunt Jenny poured me a cup of coffee, and when I finished drinking it, the grounds in the bottom of the cup spelled out trouble, misery, and death."

"That's Aunt Jenny's coffee for you," I said. She didn't rise to it.

"Ben," she said. "I'm worried about Charity."

"What?"

"She might be next," said Subrinea. "As a warning to you and as a punishment to me. Will you send her away?"

"Have you seen her tonight?"

"No. But I'm serious, Ben. There really *is* evil abroad in this place. I'm sorry now that I asked her to come here."

"Don't you worry about us. We know how to take care of ourselves." I hoped that I was right.

"The tokens don't lie," she said. The women

around her, seemingly deaf to what we were saying, hummed tunelessly.

"In the morning," I said, "I intend to have a long talk with Judge Jasper Holland. I think this news of the nuclear plant may give him something to work with. Whatever evil's abroad here is prompted by somebody who wants to make a bundle of money. And that, we can put a stop to."

She didn't seem to care. I lifted the veil to kiss her cheek, and then went upstairs to look for Charity. my room was empty, but the shower in the hall was running.

"That you, baby?" I called, opening the door.

"Yes," she said, above the sound of spraying water. "I overslept. I'll be right down. What's happening?"

I told her.

"It sounds like Subrinea's shed whatever thin coat of sophistication college gave her and reverted to a real rootstock hill woman."

"You ought to see her face," I said. I reached inside the shower curtain to give her a blind pinch. My fingers caught a warm breast, slippery with soap, and she let out a squeal.

"You ought to see *mine*, you louse!" she spluttered under the water.

I grinned and went downstairs. On the way down I heard the telephone ringing, and as I turned the corner from the landing, I saw Subrinea replacing the receiver. Before I could speak with her, she hurried down the hall and rushed from the house through the back door. I ran after her and caught up just as she got into her little Riley.

"Where are you going, Subrinea?"

"Just don't stand in my way!"

"I'm not. Remember? I'm here to help you. Now, give."

"A—man just called. He said he has information about Daddy's murder. He said he'd give it to me."

"Why didn't he give it to you on the phone?"

"I don't know. He said to meet him up on the Blood Mountain Road.

"Where?"

"It's a dirt road that goes up past the track and zigzags back and forth up to the crest of the hill behind Daddy's property." She tried to push past me.

"Hold on," I said. "I'll come with you."

"I don't know . . ." she began, but by then I was in the front seat. She hesitated, then switched on the motor and roared off, spraying gravel fifty feet behind us.

We went down to the main highway, drove to-ward Gethsemane for a few minutes, then turned left up a dirt road. At no time did the Riley ever get under fifty. Subrinea was a girl who knew how to drive. She made the turns racing style, letting up on the gas until she was well into the curve, then floor-boarding it and letting the rear end drift around.

We flashed past a black object half blocking the road. Another car.

"Baby," I said, "I think we've been had." Behind us a pair of headlights went on. "Is there a turnoff from this road?"

"I don't think so," she said, reaching over and switching off her own lights. At first I didn't think she would be able to hold the road, but with the light of the moon and the darker shadows of the bushes on both sides, she managed to ride the crown of the dirt ruts.

The car behind us was coming up fast. I looked for a turnoff. It was wasted time.

Naturally my pistol was back at the house in my suitcase, safely protected from the evil night air.

"Subrinea," I said, "the next curve we go around, get this car out into the bushes. Maybe they'll go past us and we can head out before they get turned around."

"I'll try," she said.

But she didn't get a chance. We roared over a hill and I saw a black shape in the road ahead. Subrinea flicked on the lights just as she hit the brakes, but it was too late. The little car turned sideways and skidded into the big tree that had been dropped as a roadblock. I was thrown clear, over the tree trunk and into a muddy creek just beyond it. I remember hitting the water, and that was all.

25

I woke up on the shore. Somehow, half-conscious, I had been able to drag myself there instead of drowning in the muddy water.

When I tried to move, pain shot up both arms. Feeling no fear but only a kind of puzzled surprise, I told my legs to move. They ignored me.

My right eye seemed to be blind. I felt for it, and discovered a wet, eyepatch-sized flap of skin hanging down from my forehead. I pressed it back where it belonged, but it wouldn't stay.

When it fell down over my eye again I passed out a second time.

I heard voices. The angels were coming for me. Cannily I decided to lie very still; maybe they would miss me and go away.

The voices went on. Then with my good eye I saw a light. Two lights. The angels had an automobile. It was parked on the other side of the creek, and in its headlights shadowy figures moved.

Drowsily I watched them. One looked familiar. She was a slim young figure dressed all in black. Then another familiar shape appeared. Tall, angular, wearing a long frock coat and a flop-brimmed hat.

It was Blind Judd. Now I recognized the other figures as members of the Unknown Tongue. They were supporting the young feminine figure.

Her name trembled in my memory, then came to me. I groaned.

Subrinea.

Was she alive? I couldn't tell. I tried to move again, and the pain ripped through my shoulders. My legs were still playing dead. I could move my left foot now, and that encouraged me. At least my spine wasn't broken.

The voices floated across the night to me.

"Whore of Babylon," came Blind Judd's voice. "No prayer, no patience, no reprieve from the harrowing of hell has kept you from your sinful ways. You will not be guided by the wisdom of God."

Subrinea made no answer.

"Make her ready," said Blind Judd.

The men began to strip her. They were curiously gentle, careful not to damage the black garments.

A man came around from the rear of the car. He was carrying what we called a Dixie container in the service—a barrel-sized vacuum bottle. He took off the lid, and I saw yellow smoke drift up, swirling in the glare of the headlights.

I had a sickening premonition of what was going to happen. My fear and anger helped me get to one knee, then my strength faded and I splashed into the creek again. I got a mouthful of the slimy water and choked on it.

By the time I was able to inch my way back onto the bank, two of the men had attached ropes to both of Subrinea's wrists and were pulling on them in opposite directions. She had sagged to her knees, and was kept upright only by the pressure of the ropes.

"God's will be done!" roared Blind Judd. "Sin—be cast out! The righteous must prevail! Woe unto you evil ones who turn your faces away from the eternal light of the Almighty. Eternal penance in the all-consuming fires of hell shall be your lot, for the patience of the Lord has been destroyed by your willful disobedience." To one of the men he said, "Guide my hands."

The man placed Blind Judd's hand on the Dixie container. He grunted as he lifted it. The odor of sulphur wafted my way became stronger. I managed to get on my hands and knees and crawled out into the water, toward the other bank. My heart was pounding in my ears and I had difficulty breathing. I slipped and went under, and when I came up, Blind Judd was standing over Subrinea

"Please, God," I croaked. "Let her be dead already!"

The container tilted and the boiling brimstone poured out. I was thrashing around in the creek trying to find bottom and the water was choking me, but as I went under, almost grateful for the blackness of the muddy creek, I heard one soaring shriek rising through the darkness. Then, floundering, I struck something with my head and felt the cold water swallow me.

26

Every time I lifted my head, waves of dizziness pushed me into semiconsciousness again. A disconnected series of pictures seemed to flash before me—twisting, meaningless images that might have been real or imagined.

The damp grass of the creek bank. The swirl of treetops silhouetted against the pale yellow moon as someone lifted me from the ground. A glare of headlights. The dim overhead light inside a car flashing out as a door clumped shut.

The vehicle was moving. I bounced against a hard surface. My will to awaken pushed the pain back and I managed to pull myself up into a slumped seat position. I was on the floor of a worn station wagon. It was bouncing along a dirt road. When I breathed unsteadily, I smelled a strange and exotic odor, like that of many spicy herbs.

I looked over the back of the driver's seat and saw the dim headlights sweeping shadows back away from the dirt road. The driver was a blob of darkness hunched over the wheel. I tried to speak, but all that came out was a dry-throated croak.

The driver half-turned his head, and I saw who he was. Uncle Uglybird.

"Man," he said, "I was rightfully concerned about you back there." He didn't stop the station wagon. If anything, he hit the gas a little harder. "I was afraid to take too long loading you in and getting out of there before those people came back. I thought you were alive, but I couldn't be sure."

I tried to crawl over the seat, but he let go of the wheel with his right hand and pressed me back.

"Once we get out of this dirt road," he said.

"What about her?" I croaked. My memory of it was like a nightmare, a fuzzed-up dream that I prayed wasn't true. "What about Subrinea?"

The station wagon lurched as he let go of the wheel. We swerved toward the shadows. Then Uncle Uglybird got the vehicle under control again and mashed the gas pedal savagely.

"Dear sweet Jesus!" His voice was ragged. "Is that who that poor woman was? Miss Subrinea? Mother of God!"

His shoulders slumped, and without hearing a sound or seeing his face, I knew the old black man was weeping.

I felt like joining him. Subrinea Boone would never make those little babies. The madness of this valley had seen to that.

"Ben," said Uncle Uglybird, "do you want me to take you to Dr. Appleyard? You need some stitches in your head."

"Can you do it?" I asked. "Don't want any questions for a little while. Got to talk with Charity before anything else."

"Yes sir," he said, "I reckon I can accommodate you."

We came out of the dirt road and turned left toward Gethsemane.

Uncle Uglybird indicated a wide place on the shoulder.

"That's where I was," he said, "changing a tire when you and Miss Subrinea went by doing sixty miles an hour and turned into Blood Mountain Road. I didn't recognize her, but you stood out good in the moonlight. I thought you was with Miss Charity. Well, before I got the tire fixed all the way, a big car came out of that road and headed off toward Gethsemane, breaking all the speed limits. I got my curiosity up and went up there to see what I could find. There wasn't no helping poor Miss Subrinea. But you were laying on the creek bank, near drowned. I almost didn't find you in the dark. I would have missed you total, except out of the night I heard a voice say, 'Let her be dead.' I went down, and there you were, half dead yourself."

We turned off the main highway again, and in a few minutes pulled up outside his cabin. Uncle Uglybird flicked off the headlights and ignition; the darkness closed in on us. Crickets and night birds serenaded us as he helped me inside and lit a kerosene lamp.

"You sit right there," he said. "I got to stop that bleeding first. We're lucky you didn't go into shock. Here, wrap up in this quilt. You got to keep warm."

He went into another room, came back with a water glass half filled with a clear liquid.

"Don't tell me," I said. "White lightning."

"The best," he said. "You sip at it nice and slow. It'll keep you from passing out."

"Or else *knock* me out," I said, and, predictably, choked on the liquor.

Uncle Uglybird put a big tool chest up on the table and opened it. An array of tiered shelves slipped up to each side, the kind that usually hold nails, nuts, and bolts. The compartments held plastic bags of dried leaves, roots, bark, and other herbs. The exotic odor I had noticed in the station wagon filled the room. This was Uncle Uglybird's yarb supply.

Under the compartments of herbs were other containers. These held modern medical tools— bandages, drugs, surgical instruments.

He tore open a paper envelope, took out what must have been a sterile cloth, and spread it out on the table. As he unpacked his tools, he said. "That's a bad cut on your forehead, Mr. Ben."

"Keep it just plain Ben," I said. "I must have caught the car window on my way out."

"You sure you want me to stitch it up for you? You go to see Doc Appleyard, you'll have less chance of a scar."

"Don't worry about the scar."

He soaked a cotton swab in what smelled like ether and dabbed at me. It smarted fiercely. I nipped at the white lightning.

"Ben," he said, "what's happening around here? Jesse Simpson—then that poor dog. Colonel Brown, and now Miss Subrinea."

The ether penetrated my wound like hot lead. I grabbed the arms of the chair and squeezed until my fingers popped. He stopped for a moment, and I relaxed a little.

"I know who did—*what* he did, to Subrinea at least. The question is, Why? I figured it had something to do with that piece of land Colonel Brown optioned behind the track. We could go out right now and get the man who murdered Subrinea. But it's the man behind him I want."

Uncle Uglybird put down the swab. It was matted with red. "Let me help," he said. "I'd consider it an honor."

"It could get messy."

"More messy than tonight?"

No, I thought. Nothing could get worse than that sight up on the Blood Mountain Road.

"This is going to smart some," he said, picking up an aerosol can. "This is compressed carbon dioxide, to freeze the skin so the stitching will be easier on you." I made a shrugging signal with my shoulders, and he spritzed my forehead with the spray from the can. It felt hot at first, then very cold, and the pain almost went away. Now I could feel the deep throbbing of a headache that had gone unnoticed in the more intense pain of the cut.

There was a light prickling sensation, nothing more, as he stitched up my wound with a curved needle held in a pair of forceps. His hand was deft and swift, and in minutes he was applying what looked like a huge plastic Band-aid to my head.

"Barring infection," he said, "you ought to have those stitches out in a week or so." He reached down and picked up the glass, drank deeply from it. "Pardon me," he said. "I usually don't take too much of this stuff myself. But I keep thinking of that poor girl up there on Blood Mountain."

"We'll all think of her for a long time," I said. "Now, if you'd like to help some more, here's what I'd like you to do."

"Anything," he said.

"Drive up to Butterfield. Bring Charity

Tucker back here. Don't tell her what's happened. Don't tell anyone."

"Not even the Law?"

"Especially not the Law," I said. "If you really want to help, Uncle Uglybird, you've got to play it my way."

"I'm on my way." He took my arm and helped me up. "Now, you just lay down a while on this cot. I'll be back before you know it. Meantime, try not to move around. You lost a lot of blood. Try to rest."

I stretched out, my mind racing. Uncle Uglybird went out quietly, and I heard the station wagon start and drive away.

"Rest?" I said out loud. Fat chance. There was too much to think about, too much planning to do. . . .

"Ben?"

A hand touched my forehead. I came back from a far-off place where I had been lying on the cool grass, counting white, fleecy clouds.

"Ben?"

I opened my eyes. Charity was looking down at me, her eyes wide and frightened.

"What happened? Oh, Ben, are you all *right*?"

I groaned as I sat up. Every muscle ached.

"Hello, baby," I said. My voice was strained and, even to my ears, weak.

Uncle Uglybird brought over a chair. "Sit here, Miss Charity," he said.

She sat and took both of my hands in hers. "Ben, what's wrong? What happened to your head? Where's Subrinea?"

I took the big one first.

"Dead," I said.

"What?"

"Subrinea's dead."

Her face didn't change. I realized we had both reached the point in this case where there was simply too much horror piled on top of more horror.

"How?" she asked. Uncle Uglybird turned and left the room.

"The same as Jesse Simpson. The same as Blue."

She stared at me for a long while. When her voice came, it was small and toneless.

"Oh, no," she said.

She stared at the ceiling. Her eyes were wide. The tears started—great, fat, rolling droplets that streaked her cheeks. She shook her head back and forth.

"Oh, no," she said again.

I touched her arm and then, quick as a snake striking, she slapped me hard. A flash of anger distorted her face.

"You let it happen!" she cried. And then, as quickly as it had appeared, the look of anger was gone. She reached out both arms like a little girl and fell toward me. I caught her, and as she sobbed against my neck, I discovered the surprising fact that hardened, tough Ben Shock was bawling right along with her, with all the uninhibited anguish of a hurt child. And what is more, it felt good! I sensed an accumulation of the strangling poison of grief, of shock, of self-recrimination draining out of my system.

A deliberate cough came from the door. Uncle Uglybird came in as we drew apart.

I decided it was time to tell them what I had seen.

When I got to Blind Judd, Charity cursed and said, "I knew it! We should have locked him up."

"On what charge? No, baby, we did all we could."

I felt I was reading her mind. She started to say, "Tell that to Subrinea!" but thought better of it. Instead, she chewed on her lip.

"I don't think Blind Judd is the end of the line," I went on. "I have strong feelings about our old buddy Mayor Hornbuckle. Not to mention Sheriff Goff. I propose we lay a trap for them."

Uncle Uglybird produced some paper when I asked for it—a dusty box of Eaton stationery, bilious-green-colored paper with deckled edges and matching envelopes.

"Lady give this to me in payment for a cure," he said.

With my ballpoint pen I printed: SUBRINEA IS TAKEN CARE OF. GO AHEAD WITH THE PLAN.

I sealed the note in one of the envelopes. "Uncle Uglybird, let's you and me pay a visit to our good Mayor. We'll slip this under his door, ring the bell, and run for it. Then we'll watch to see how he reacts."

"He won't fall for it," said Charity.

"What do you suggest?" I snapped.

"You'll just warn him that we know something," she said.

"Who's 'we'? The note's not signed."

Charity sighed. She was still in a near state of shock.

"We'll drop you at Butterfield," I said.

"Not on your life," she said. "I'm in this all the way."

I was still shaky, but I managed to stay on my legs all the way out to my Fleetwood, which Charity had driven to Uncle Uglybird's. I sank gratefully into the front seat, Charity slid in beside me, and we bounced through the night toward Mayor Oppie Hornbuckle's house on the hill.

27

There were lights on inside Hornbuckle's house. I hoped he was alone, free from the companionship of any stray ladies with whips.

We parked the car well down the hill, motor running. Charity sat behind the wheel while Uncle Uglybird and I went up the hill.

"You're not moving too well, Ben," he said. "Let me do this."

I wanted to argue, but I knew he was right. As I watched, he slipped up onto the porch and tucked the note under the front door. Then he pressed the doorbell twice and dived for the shadows. He moved very fast for an old man.

In a few seconds the door opened. It was Hornbuckle. He looked around, blinking into the darkness. Seeing no one, he started to close the door. Then he looked down and saw the note. He bent and picked it up. He looked at both sides of the envelope, then out into the darkness again. His thumb ripped open the seal and he took out the square of green paper.

He read the note, dropped it to his side, and came out to the edge of the porch.

"Who's out there?" he called. At that moment Uncle Uglybird came out of the bushes and touched my arm.

"Let's get going," he said.

We hightailed it down the road. Behind us Mayor Hornbuckle called again, "Who are you?"

Back at the car, parked safely out of sight behind a hedge, we waited. Minutes passed.

"Maybe he's checking it out on the phone," said Charity.

"And risk the operator listening in? I doubt it," I said. I hoped I was right.

We heard the car coming long before the headlights lit up the trees that lined the road. The Mayor was driving like the demons of hell were behind him.

"Follow him," I said unnecessarily. When Hornbuckle's car roared past us, we slipped out, headlights dark, and drove through the cloud of dust he had left.

"He's going into town," Charity said when we reached the main highway.

We got as close to him as we dared. I hoped he wasn't going to the courthouse. That would have told us precisely nothing.

He skidded his car to a stop outside a low white building.

"Ben!" said Charity. "That's Loyal's office."

"I know."

The station wagon slid silently under the shadow of a tree across the street. We watched. Hornbuckle got out of his car, looked nervously around, and tapped at Loyal Boone's door.

"I don't believe it," Charity said.

The door opened. The Mayor said something, and then went inside.

"Let's go," I said.

We hurried across the street. The door was unlocked. I eased it open.

"Better take this," said Charity. She slipped me the thin .25 automatic she carries in her purse.

It felt tiny in my hand, but the coldness of its metal comforted me.

We crept through the hall. The rising and falling of arguing voices came from Loyal's office.

At the door, which was opened a crack, we waited and listened.

"Making money's one thing, Loyal," said Hornbuckle's voice. "But this! I swear I don't know anything about it."

Loyal's voice, when it came, was choked.

"You bastard," he said, "I'll break your neck if you don't tell the truth. Where did you get this? What's happened to Subrinea?"

"I don't know," said Hornbuckle. "Someone

left it on my porch. Loyal, I swear to you all I was mixed up in was a land deal. We were harassing the Colonel to keep him from opening the track, but that's purely all there was to it."

"What about Jesse Simpson?" Loyal asked.

"I don't know the first thing about that, Loyal." There was a choking noise, and then the Mayor said, "Let me go, boy! I'm telling you the truth."

I stepped inside.

"Let him go, Loyal," I said. "Let's hear what he has to say."

Loyal started, released Hornbuckle. He stepped toward me.

"Ben," he said, his voice strained, "what's happened to Subrinea?"

I didn't like myself, but I said, "Let's hear what the Mayor's got to say first."

Hornbuckle, who had staggered to the leather sofa, said, "So help me, Mr. Shock, all this violence and mystery has me just as puzzled as you are. That's why I came right here when I got this note. Jesse Simpson and the Colonel were bad enough—but if something's happened to Miss Subrinea, I don't want any part of it."

Loyal started to say something, but I cut him off. "Who do you think is behind it?"

"Not the Sheriff," Hornbuckle said. "He was taking orders from me. He didn't even know who put the money behind the deal."

"The deal to void that option? So you could

get the land the Power Commission wants for the nuclear power plant?"

"Yes," he said, licking his lips. "We didn't mean anybody any harm, we just wanted that plot of land."

"Then why did you come here?"

"Because maybe I figured him wrong. Maybe he's been going around me, maybe he's got something to do with these murders. And if he has, I don't want any part of it."

"Who's 'he,' Mayor?" I asked.

He looked at me, blinking. "I thought you knew. Senator Treffit, of course."

"Did you and the Senator have any dealings with Blind Judd and the Unknown Tongue?"

"Those fanatics? Of course not."

"Are you sure the Senator couldn't have without your knowing it?"

"Maybe. Why?"

Loyal grabbed my arm. "Yes, Ben—why?"

I told him about Subrinea.

28

Charity wanted to take Loyal back to Butterfield, but he insisted on going with us.

"You go ahead, baby," I said. "Get Aunt Jenny to send Chuck Wallace and a couple of the other men from Butterfield up there on the mountain. Somebody ought to bring her home."

"I'll take care of everything," she said. She pressed my hand and climbed into Loyal's car.

In the station wagon Loyal said, "She said she saw a death token in the coffee grounds tonight. I shouldn't have taken my eyes off her. But what did I do? I got drunk!" The pain in his face was more than I could look at.

Hornbuckle seemed even more nervous as we drove toward the Senator's house, out on the main Lexington highway.

"Have you got anything else you want to say?" I asked.

"No," he said. "Nothing."

There were several cars parked in the Senator's driveway. One was a blue Porsche. If Loyal noticed it, he said nothing.

The Senator himself opened the door. He started to say, "Counselor Boone, what a—" and that was as far as he got before Loyal nailed him with a vicious right to the gut. The Senator went "Whoomph!" and sat down heavily.

"Help me up with him," said Loyal. We took Treffit's arms and half-dragged him into the living room. There were two drinks on the coffee table, but the room was empty.

"You bastard," said Loyal, "if you don't talk straight, I'm going to kill you. Do you understand me?"

"Jesus Christ, boy," gasped the Senator, "I think you already *ruptured* me."

"Osgood," said the Mayor, "I told them the truth. I had to."

"You *had* to?" said the Senator. "What do you mean, you *had* to?"

Before Hornbuckle could answer, Loyal grabbed Treffit by the throat. "Damn you," he shouted, "don't mess around with me. My wife is dead, burned to death. The Mayor says you're the man behind a conspiracy to overthrow Colonel Brown's option on that Blood Mountain land behind the track. Speak up. Is that right?"

"Well, son," began the Senator, trying to smile. He didn't finish. Loyal broke his nose with a piledriver punch that made a cracking sound I heard from across the room. Bright red blood cascaded down Treffit's shirt. Frightened, he grabbed a handkerchief and tried to stanch the flow.

"I asked you a question," Loyal said.

"Don't beat up that old man any more," said a voice behind us.

We turned.

It was Harmon Boone.

He came over and picked up one of the drinks on the coffee table.

"I'm sorry, son," he said. "Treffit wasn't the real man behind this. He just located the nuclear power plant deal for us. I'm the one who tried to force Adger out."

Loyal made an inarticulate growl in his throat and flung himself at his father. Harmon threw the drink in his son's face and tripped him with one foot. Before Loyal could move, Harmon Boone had twisted his arm around behind his back and held him helpless.

"Don't do any permanent damage," I warned, showing Charity's little .25 pistol.

"Don't worry," said Harmon. Then, to his son: "Can I let you up, Loyal?"

Loyal nodded his head. Harmon released the pressure.

"Son," said Harmon, "I'm just as sorry as I can

be about the way this all turned out. It isn't what I had in mind."

"What did you have in mind?" I asked.

"The usual sordid tale," he said. "When the Senator found out about the power plant and brought his scheme to Oppie Hornbuckle, they needed someone on the inside of the Colonel's operation to help out."

"I thought he was your friend," I said.

"He was," said Harmon. "But, boy, you got to understand that this is awful big money we're talking about."

"What he means," Hornbuckle put in anxiously, "is that we didn't have nothing to do with those killings."

"Are you one hundred percent sure of that?" I asked.

"On my word of honor as a state senator," said Treffit, dabbing at his bleeding nose with the reddened handkerchief. "We got a little money hungry. We even fiddled around with equipment out at the track to give Adger a hard time with his suppliers and hold up the opening. I'll admit it, we were trying to starve him out. But murder? No!"

Oddly, I believed him. "How about your faithful watchdog Sheriff Goff?"

"He wouldn't do anything like that on his own," said Hornbuckle.

"Call him. Get him out here."

He dialed, said something quietly into the receiver. Then he hung up. "He's not in the office."

"Let me have that phone." I asked the operator to connect me with the Brown home. Aunt Jenny answered.

"Miss Charity ain't here," she said. "She said to tell you she was going out to talk with Mrs. Boone."

"Maria Boone?" I asked. As far as Aunt Jenny knew, there were still two Mrs. Boones. It was obvious from her tone of voice that Charity had not told her about Subrinea.

"Yes, sir. She said to tell you she'd found out something about a man named Mendoza."

I thanked her and hung up. So. Hector Mendoza, Maria's cousin, was mixed up in this, too.

"I think," I said. "that we ought to get all of this information down before a stenographer. That is"—and I looked straight at Harmon Boone—"unless you've all decided to deny everything and wait for your lawyers' instructions."

"No need for that," said Harmon.

"We just want to be kept out of this murder business," said Hornbuckle.

"Let's go," I said.

We piled into the various cars and started off toward Gethsemane.

Near the courthouse I saw something that made me slam on the brakes.

"You stay with them and keep them honest," I told Loyal as I slipped out the left front door of the Fleetwood. Puzzled, he slid behind the wheel.

I went around the corner fast. I had seen a familiar figure letting himself into the darkened front entrance of Judge Jasper Holland.

Now what, I wondered, would Blind Judd have to discuss with the judge?

I didn't see any of his followers around. But they obviously wouldn't be very far away.

The door was unlocked. I slipped it open and went inside quickly.

Blind Judd was on his knees behind the judge's desk, rummaging through the drawers. He started up as I entered, almost as if he could see me. I stepped back and switched on the light.

I took out Charity's .25.

"Preacher," I said, "in case you don't recognize my voice, this is Ben Shock. I saw what happened up there on the Blood Mountain Road. So if you don't think I'll shoot you just because you're blind, think again."

The door behind Blind Judd opened. I saw the judge groping his way into the room.

"Get back, Judge!" I yelled. But I was too late. Blind Judd grabbed the old man and tugged his slight body in front of his own.

"Fire your puny weapon," Blind Judd shouted, pushing Judge Holland toward me as a living shield. "On your head be the sin! You have joined these sinners in defending the Devil's playground, and you shall be destroyed just as those who created it were destroyed!"

I edged away from him, trying to get an angle. He seemed to anticipate my moves.

"Ben!" called Judge Holland. "The radio! Turn it on!"

I realized that Blind Judd was zeroing in on me with that peculiar kind of sonic radar that blind people sometimes develop. I found the radio, switched it on, then threw it down behind a cabinet. No sound came from it.

Blind Judd shoved Judge Holland to one side. The old man smashed into the edge of a door and crumpled to the floor.

I raised my pistol. But I couldn't bring myself to shoot the blind man after all. I tried to creep up on him, to slug him one, but he heard me coming and lashed out with a foot that caught me in the pit of the stomach. I went one way and the pistol went another. Now we were worse than even. I tried not to breathe.

Blind Judd stood in the center of the room, head tilted to one side, listening.

I tried to get up on one knee.

He heard me, grimaced, and moved toward me.

I rolled out of distance. I tried to locate the pistol, but it was nowhere to be seen. At that moment I would gladly have overcome my previous reluctance and blasted off a couple of kneecaps.

257

He turned toward me. His hand went to his belt and came back holding a knife that would have turned Jim Bowie green with envy. He waved it in little circles as he advanced on me.

He was talking quietly under his breath now, most of the words swallowed up, but a few coming through loud and clear. "Son of Satan . . . God's will be done . . ."

Just when I had given up completely on any help from the radio, it warmed up and came to life. The heavy thump of a rock number blared from its speaker. Although my musical tastes run more to Ella Fitzgerald, nothing had ever sounded so good.

Blind Judd stopped, puzzled. He did not react when I got to my feet. He began to move toward the radio, obviously unable to hear anything else. I picked up a heavy metal trophy. It was a thoroughbred horse in full gallop, and I later discovered that the inscription read, "For a true friend of the King of Sports, presented by the Kentucky Racing Association to Judge Jasper Holland."

I gave Blind Judd a nice whack across the wrist with the horse's head. The knife clattered to the floor and I kicked it away. He turned toward me and I made ready to give him the thoroughbred against the noggin.

I had not been aware of the door opening, but someone caught at my arm and almost got belted in the jaw for her pains. It was the girl from the Unknown Tongue church, Blind Judd's daughter.

"Don't hit him!" she cried.

When he heard her voice, Blind Judd almost staggered. "Mary!" he called, "is that you?"

She caught his right hand in both of her own. "It's me, Daddy," she said. "Now you got to sit down and be quiet. Please."

He let her lead him to a chair. Loyal, who had also entered unnoticed, was helping Judge Holland to his feet. Harmon stood at the door, looking embarrassed.

"Please don't hurt my daddy," said Mary. "He's not responsible."

"Is that why you sent me to see Brother Randolph?" I asked.

She nodded. "I didn't want to come right out and tell tales on my daddy, but I was hoping someone would find out about him and put him in a hospital where he belongs before he . . ." She looked down.

"Before he killed again?" I said gently. She nodded. "Well, I'm afraid we didn't make it, Miss Mary. Do you know what happened up on Blood Mountain tonight?"

She shook her head. I told her, and she began to weep quietly.

"What about Adger?" asked Harmon. "Was he responsible for that, too?"

"I placed the instrument of the Lord in the

259

bed of that sinner!" boomed Blind Judd. "And the Lord struck him down."

"Not quite," I said, "Somebody helped the good Lord along." Looking at Loyal, I added. "and it just doesn't sound like Blind Judd's work. I'll buy him for Jesse Simpson, and we all know about Subrinea."

"There's Blue," said Harmon suddenly. Loyal gave him a disgusted look.

"How about the dog?" I asked Mary. "Did your father wire him up and use brimstone on the animal too? And why?"

"Wire?" said Loyal. "I didn't see any wire."

"Somebody used it," I said. "Then when it was all over, they removed it."

"Blue wasn't much of a dog," said Loyal, "but he wouldn't have set there and let anyone he didn't know wire him up."

"Who could have done it?" I asked.

"I could have," Loyal said. He looked at his father. "And *he* could have. So could Maria."

"We were all having dinner when it happened," said his father.

"No," I reminded him. "Someone left the table."

"My God," said Harmon. "Maria?"

I felt fear grab at my stomach. Quickly I told them of Charity's message about Hector Mendoza. I had been worried when I heard where she had gone, but had counted on Maria's presence to keep the danger to a minimum. If *she* was mixed up in this thing, all bets were off.

We stashed Blind Judd in the jail and managed to rout out three deputies. Sheriff Goff arrived in the middle of our preparations and joined the expedition. In several cars we set off toward the Boone house.

Coming down the long straightaway just before the curve that twisted above the Boone property, the lead car with the three deputies in it came under fire from the darkness and slewed off the road.

Sheriff Goff was seated next to me in the Fleetwood. "Got the front tires," he said. We skidded to a stop. The deputies crawled for cover, shaken but uninjured.

Harmon's Porsche behind us stopped and he came up to join us. Loyal sat behind the wheel, his face grim and tense.

"There," said Goff, pointing.

One of the roofs of the Boone estate stuck up just high enough over the crest of the hill to give a group of men a vantage point. They were crouched on the roof.

"What's the matter with them?" said Harmon. He ran down the road, yelling and waving his arms. "It's me!" he called. "Hold your fire! You're making a mistake." They opened up on him. As bullets threw up dust at his feet, he dived for shelter in the ditch.

The deputies rejoined us. "We can't get a clear shot at them," one said.

"We don't need a clear shot," said Goff. "I'm gonna crawl up there with this here Armalite gun. It'll go right through the roof."

I recognized the riot control weapon. It was reputed to be able to shoot through a brick wall.

"Will that thing shoot through an engine block?" I asked.

Goff grinned, and I knew I'd found my crow sniper.

"I can thread a needle with this here thing," he said. "You wasn't ever in any danger."

"I suppose Hornbuckle put you up to it."

"Sure enough. Sorry, he had some idea you could be scared off."

"We can settle all this later," I said. Loyal had joined us and overheard the last part of the conversation.

"You'll never get close enough," he said. "They've got a field of fire right down the middle of this road."

"What else you got to suggest?" asked Goff.

"Watch," said Loyal. He dashed back to the little Porsche, started the motor and roared up alongside us. "Give me a couple of seconds, and then come in fast," he said.

"Hold on there," began Goff, but Loyal was already screeching rubber against the hard clay of the road.

He was doing forty-five by the time he passed the overturned deputy's car.

"He'll never make that curve," said Goff.

"I don't think he intends to," I said, dragging the sheriff into the Fleetwood.

I couldn't see the details in the darkness—only the red tail lights of the Porsche as it headed into the curve. Instead of arcing around to the left, it kept going straight. It bounced high in the air as it hit a ditch at the edge of the road, then curved, missile-like, through the air, headed straight for the roof where the snipers crouched. There was a leaden, crunching sound as the Porsche struck the roof, and then the car, roof, and men were engulfed in an exploding blossom of gasoline flames.

"Let's go!" said Goff, and I put my foot down on the gas. I was barely able to stop before running him down. He ripped open the rear door and piled in.

"Loyal got out of the car all right," he gasped, pointing to a clump of bushes at the edge of the road. "He's over there."

I saw nothing. Besides, there was no time.

We made the run down into the alley in record time. The compound gate was open. Inside, total confusion. Men with clothing afire were crawling out of the burning building. Getting them into custody was more of a rescue operation than an arrest.

I grabbed a handcuffed Mexican and pushed him up against the Fleetwood.

"Where's the blond señorita who came up here to talk with Senora Boone?"

He shrugged. *"No hablo inglés, señor."*

I reached over and plucked a .38 from the holster of one of the deputies and jammed it into the Mexican's mouth. He tried to shut his teeth over the barrel and ended spitting out two incisors.

I held up three fingers and began counting out loud. *"Uno. Dos. Tr—"*

He was so eager to talk that he sprayed me with a mixture of blood and spit.

"They go to snake farm. Up *montana de sangre, comprende?*"

I comprehended. My girl had got suckered into that abominable snake farm on Blood Mountain.

Harmon was wandering around the burning wreckage of his estate like a lost soul.

"Where are the horses?" I demanded. "They've got Charity."

"But why?" he asked. "Why would Hector be involved in this? He knew nothing about the power plant—and couldn't have benefited even if he had."

"Don't ask me," I said. "If I were that poor blind madman back there in Gethsemane, I'd be inclined to say you were getting a little of the harrowing of hell yourself, to pay you back for the lousy deal you pulled on Adger and Subrinea."

As we harnessed the horses, Harmon said, "That building's built like a fortress. I know. I designed it. You'd never get in there by yourself. But I can work it."

Goff stared at him. "Why would you want to?"

"He—Hector—has Maria."

"Maybe," I said.

"I'm going," he said.

Goff looked at me. I shrugged. "Let him come. He knows the trail better than anyone else anyway."

We mounted up, looking like a ragtag guerrilla force, and set off up the trail to the Unknown Tongue village and Harmon Boone's snake farm.

29

Although there were only kerosene lanterns in the Unknown Tongue village, their light helped us pick our way along the narrow trail until we came to a group of people standing in our path.

One woman stepped forward and addressed Sheriff Goff. "Where is our preacher?"

"In jail," said Goff. There was a murmur from the group and they moved toward us. "No offense, ma'am," the sheriff went on, "but Blind Judd's as nutty as a fruitcake." He patted his pistol. "Now, we got business on up the hill, so if you folks will stand aside?"

They grumbled, but they moved back. Goff left one deputy there to keep an eye on our rear, and then we tied up the horses. Somehow, in the next few minutes, the only real mountain man among us took charge.

"Ben and me'll go up first," Harmon said. "Give us ten minutes, then come up the trail. Keep your tails down. You may draw some fire."

I swapped my borrowed .38 for Sheriff Goff's Armalite gun. Firing a tiny rocket projectile, the Armalite was the nearest thing to a bazooka you could get.

Without any farewells, Harmon padded off into the darkness. I followed him, banging my shins on fallen trees and slipping on rolling pebbles.

It was two minutes short of the ten Harmon had asked for when we came up on the back end of the snake farm building. I was wheezing like a foundered horse, though Harmon seemed to be breathing normally.

"We'll never get inside in time," said Harmon. "I hope Goff listened to me and keeps his ass down."

"What now?"

For answer he ducked down in the bushes. I followed. A man came around the corner of the building. The T-shirted Mexican I had seen on my first visit. He carried an automatic shotgun.

I heard dogs barking in the distance and checked my watch. Ten minutes to the second.

The Mexican reacted. He looked around, then slid a key into the back door of the snake farm building and went inside.

"You didn't tell Goff anything about dogs," I said.

Harmon shrugged. "As long as he keeps his tail down he'll be all right. Meanwhile, we've got a nice little diversion."

I heard the heavy crumping of rifle fire. It sounded like an elephant hunt. Those Mexicans weren't using .22s.

We slid up against the building like shadows against a pavement. The moon painted the walls with silver fingers.

Harmon listened with his ear against the door for a moment. Then he slid a key into the lock and the door swung open. I went in fast. He followed me.

The room was empty except for glass cages—some containing snakes—packing crates, and shipping materials. There was a door at the far end. Harmon started for it, but I held him back. There was a ventilating grille above it. I pushed a crate over and climbed up, trying not to wheeze from the effort.

I was right. The T-shirted Mexican had heard us after all. He was outside the door, waiting in a crouch, the shotgun pointed at the doorknob. I slid down to the floor and took a prone position behind the crate. I raised the Armalite in both hands. drew a bead on the spot behind the door where I estimated the guard's belly button to be, and squeezed the trigger.

A hole the size of a garbage-can lid exploded out of the doorway.

I was admiring it when the door swung open. I

saw the Mexican had put a sixteen-gauge load of buckshot through it in a reflexive action when the Armalite round struck him.

The hole it had made in his stomach didn't approach the size of the buckshot pattern, but it was big enough to put him out of action forever.

Harmon leaped over me and drew a bead on the room with his own rifle. I scrambled to my feet and joined him.

"Drop it!" I heard Harmon yell, and then I saw Hector Mendoza turning toward us with a deer rifle in his hands. He started to bring it to bear. Harmon fired first. Mendoza's face dissolved into a red mask and he was slammed backward into a row of snake cages.

The Mexicans who had been firing through the windows at the approaching lawmen threw down their weapons and advanced toward us, hands raised, spewing barrages of anxious Spanish into the air.

"Beautifully done, my husband," said a woman's voice behind us, "but you are too late."

I whirled. Tied to a chair in the center of the sand-filled arena the snake handlers had used for milking the reptiles, Charity looked at me with terrified eyes. Maria Boone stood near her, holding a glass cage. Inside it was the brightly colored New Guinea coral snake.

"Come on, Maria," said Harmon. "What do you want to hurt that girl for? We can talk this out."

"We have never talked anything out!" she said. "The grave has always been between us!"

"Now, that's not my fault, Maria," he said, moving toward her. She opened the lid of the cage a little and he stopped. "Now, talk reason, Maria. I never hurt you no way that I know."

"You poor fool," she said softly. "You always believed that story about the rattlesnake bite . . . and about me being lost in the desert. Has it never occurred to you that I was waiting there for you?"

"No," he said, "it never has."

"Do you remember my father?"

"Of course I do. Señor Mendoza—"

"He was *not* my father, Harmon. I was his woman, and he tired of me, but he still felt affection for me and so we designed a plan to bring the rich *gringo* to our home. I was what you call a chattel. All the Mendozas had me whenever they wanted."

Harmon's voice was hard. "Even Hector?"

"Especially Hector," she said.

"What grave was there between us?"

"Yours," she said. "You were to die long before now. But somehow everything went wrong. Do you remember being so ill in Mexico City? My husband, you consumed enough arsenic to destroy a regiment. And what did it do to you?"

"I thought I had the *turistas*," Harmon said. "So that's all there ever was? My money?"

"What else? Do you think any woman, even a

271

poor Mexican, would have wanted you for what you were?"

I had been trying to inch my way toward the fence around the snake pit. She shot a glance at me. "No further, Mr. Shock," she said.

Charity had been listening to all this without any sign of hearing. Now she lifted her head and looked directly at me. It was like staring into the wrong end of a telescope. She wavered and receded before my eyes until I felt as if I were going to lose my balance and pitch forward on my face.

"But why the killing?" Harmon made half a step toward the snake pit, and I shuddered as Maria almost dumped the coral snake out onto Charity's bare neck.

"Have you ever heard of a plant called *Cannabis sativa?*" she asked.

"Hemp?" he said. "Marihuana?"

"Precisely. Where do you think my—protector, Senor Mendoza, got his fortune? So he decided to send his son, Hector, to Kentucky with me, to engage in the same business."

"That doesn't explain the killings," I said.

"But it does," she said. "Hector was afraid that someone would stumble on our planting fields. He said that people must be kept away from Blood Mountain."

"And Blind Judd listened to him," I said. "He told that crazed man stories about sin and damnation, and Blind Judd went out and killed for him?" I stopped looking at Charity. I knew, we all knew, our only chance was to ask questions, keep her talking, buy time until somebody could think of something to do.

I was close enough to the fence for a wild dive, but I didn't know what I'd be able to do if I got over it.

"Yes," she said. "At first I knew nothing of it. We were frightened of Adger Brown, of what would happen if he exercised that land option and began developing Blood Mountain. We weren't interested in marihuana itself. That is too plentiful and too cheap. Instead, the crops were refined into hashish."

"How could anyone miss a couple of fields of marihuana?" I asked.

"They were scattered around the mountain," she said. "When they were harvested, Hector's men worked here at the snake farm to do the processing."

"And," I said, "you handled your shipping by packing the stuff in with live snakes. What postal inspector was ever going to check out those boxes?"

She nodded. "But then, when the racetrack began, things got out of hand. I did not know it at the time, but Hector brought Blind Judd in to keep the Unknown Tongue under control. Then he began using them for his murder plans. Blind Judd put a copperhead in Adger Brown's bed and brought on Adger's heart attack. Later, when Jesse Simpson discovered a marihuana patch just outside the track property, he talked around town about something strange he'd found, and Hector knew immediately what it was. By then he and Blind Judd had worked out the brimstone method of 'purifying' sinners, and all he had to do was convince Blind Judd and his followers that Jesse Simpson was an evildoer, mixed up with Satan and the racetrack."

"I saw what happened to Subrinea," I said. "That took a little while. How did they work it with Jesse Simpson? Chuck Wallace heard Jesse scream."

"They killed Simpson somewhere else and took him to the barn," she said. "Hector screamed, and they left the body there to be found."

"Simple," I said, taking out the notebook Simpson's widow had given to Loyal. Inside was what I had thought was poinsettia. I showed it to Harmon. "Don't tell me that this is a marihuana leaf."

He looked at it and nodded.

I sighed. "That's what comes of being a city boy. And that's why they sent Blind Judd to Judge Holland's. He was handling Simpson's affairs and they thought *he* had it. Look, Maria, why don't you come on over here where we can talk?"

She shook her head. "I can see what you have in your mind. And I see what Sheriff Goff is planning. Do not attempt it, Sheriff. Even if a bullet should strike me, this coral snake will fall on Miss Tucker's neck."

"Why the dog?" I asked.

"I always hated the beast," she said. "And I felt it would be even more effective with Loyal than Simpson's death."

"What about the option papers?"

She looked puzzled. Harmon scuffed his foot on the cement floor. "Actually," he said, "*we* got those papers out of there the day before. Me and Hornbuckle."

"So, Maria, you slapped away from the table when we were having dinner," I said, "and wired up Blue so he couldn't bark or howl, and Hector Mendoza gave him the brimstone treatment."

"That's right," she said. "Hector was wondrously efficient at killing. When he went to Lexington to be sure Adger Brown would never come home, he posed as an attendant, drugged the night nurse, and injected copperhead venom into the old man with a hypodermic."

"And what about Subrinea?" I prodded. I was another few feet closer to the fence.

A different look came into her eyes. "I had nothing to do with that," she said. "When Hector heard about the memorial race she was scheduling, he went away on his own. I would never have hurt that girl."

"Sure," I said. "Simpson and Adger were men,

275

and Blue was only a dog. But you'd never hurt a girl."

"I do not care if you believe me or not," she said.

Somebody had to make a move, and it looked like I was elected. The Armalite gun was crooked in my arm. I started to turn toward Harmon, saying, "Listen, she's your wife—"and as the gun came to bear, I squeezed off three fast rounds. Two missed. The third smashed the glass cage, and the coral snake dropped to the sand.

Maria shouted something in Spanish and threw the remains of the cage away from her. Meanwhile the snake, no fool he, was heading for the far distances of the pit's corner. Still screaming, Maria grabbed the little reptile by the tail and lifted it to throw at Charity.

Almost faster than the eye could follow, the snake twisted its body and fastened itself onto Maria's wrist. She dropped the tail, but now the snake was held on firmly by the clamp of its own jaws. Harmon and I both leaped over the fence. I made a dive at Charity and gave her seated figure as good a body block as you'd ever see at the Super Bowl. We both tumbled a good three yards away from Maria and her ghastly burden.

Harmon slapped the coral snake with one hand and it writhed against the fence. One of the deputies leaned over and smashed it into the sand with the butt of his rifle.

"I told you the grave was between us," Maria said, almost whispering. Then she fell. Harmon tried to catch her, but missed, and when he drew her up there was moist sand clinging to her motionless cheek.

30

You don't want to go to the funerals, but you do. You have had a hand in the paths and events that led toward the grave, and there is no way to escape without paying a final obeisance to the dark forces that brought these things to pass.

Adger and Subrinea were buried on the same day. The sun was bright, and all through the service a noisy murder of crows perched in a nearby tree and commented on the proceedings. They sounded angry, which suited my mood perfectly. Charity was crying, and I wanted a drink. What a lousy goddamned business, I thought.

As we left the cemetery, Loyal handed me a thin brown envelope.

"Funny," he said as I tucked it in my pocket. "They got what they wanted. The track's never going to open. I couldn't stand to look at it."

"You sure you want to pay us?" I asked. "We weren't very damned helpful."

"You did your job," he said. "Those maniacs might have gotten two or three more of us if you hadn't been around. You don't have anything to feel sorry about. Far from it."

I didn't agree. But then nothing is perfect. Charity came up and took my arm from behind.

"We've got to be going, Ben," she said. I could tell from her voice how badly she needed to get away from this place.

"Where's your father?" I asked Loyal.

"Putting his—putting Maria's body on the train," he said. "Along with Hector Mendoza's. It seems the old man down there wanted them sent to Mexico for burial."

"Good!" said Charity, and I welcomed the note of vengeance in her voice. Good, I echoed inwardly. Who the hell says you have to keep turning the other cheek?

"Brother Randolph has taken over the Unknown Tongue sect again," Loyal said. "He says they'll move closer to the valley, in time."

Up in the tree the crows cawed their opinion. It wasn't very favorable.

"Then that's just about it," I said, leading Charity out toward the Fleetwood—all packed and ready to get us the hell out of the bluegrass country.

"Nothing left," said Loyal. He held out his

hand. I shook it. Charity wrapped her arms around his neck and gave him a tearful kiss.

"So long," I said.

He didn't answer. He was looking over my shoulder.

Harmon Boone got out of the Fleetwood. He came over and stood in front of his son. His shoulders were slumped and he looked a thousand years old.

"Son," he said. "I'm real sorry."

Loyal's hands trembled. For a moment I thought he was going to strike his father. Then his arms relaxed and his eyes softened. He made half a step toward Harmon and put his hands up and then the two men hugged in that brusque, masculine way that you only see in times of tragedy.

"Daddy," said Loyal. "Daddy, we're both alone now."

"We got you and me," said Harmon.

They drew apart, embarrassed.

"There's my car," said Loyal.

"That's good," said Harmon. "If I recollect, you demolished mine."

They went to Loyal's car, got in and drove away. Charity was bawling.

I helped her into the Fleetwood.

"Just to ease my mind," I said, "where did you get the lead on Hector?"

"Your buddy Chief Harlon Caldwell called from Lexington," she said. "Someone saw him at the hospital, and he wanted you to check Hector out for him."

"Well," I said, turning onto the main road, "we did that."

"Yes," she said, "we did that."

I handed her the envelope. "Our fee," I said.

"How much?"

"I don't know," I said. "I'm just not interested right now."

She stuck it in her purse. "Neither am I."

We stopped in at Uncle Jeff's and drank one too many pitchers of his home brew. Charity had to skip out to the john and came back with her eyes raw and red.

"Shock," she said, "we've got to stop getting involved with our clients."

"Amen."

"Rule number one," she said.

"*Numero uno*," I agreed.

We drove over to the Lexington highway. I stopped at the red sign and threw the blinkers onto right turn position.

"What's up that way?" she asked.

"Lexington. The turnpike. New York."

"Turn left," she said.

I turned left.

"What's down this way?" I asked.

"Mississippi," she said. "The Gulf Coast. Great skin diving."

"What else?"

"Some trouble on a Texas Tower," she said. "Off-shore drilling, oil, that bit."

"Do I have any choice?" I asked.

"No."

"Okay," I sighed, "here we go."

We went. Behind us the crows cawed their goodbyes.

MORE MYSTERY FROM STEIN AND DAY

			U.S.	CAN.
8128-1	**AS MERRY AS HELL** John Creasey		2.95	
8026-9	**DEATH IN THE CARIBBEAN** John R.L. Anderson		2.95	NCR
8112-5	**DEATH IN THE CHANNEL** John R.L. Anderson		2.95	3.50
8162-1	**DEATH IN THE NORTH SEA** John R.L. Anderson		2.95	3.50
8014-5	**THE DIANE GAME** Stanley Cohen		3.50	3.50
8152-4	**FLOOD** Lionel Black		2.95	
8107-9	**HONOR THY GODFATHER** Thomas P. Mulkeen		2.95	3.50
8171-0	**THE LIFE AND DEATH OF PETER WADE** Lionel Black		2.95	NCR
8032-3	**MAN ON A SHORT LEASH** Kenneth Royce		2.95	

MORE MYSTERY FROM STEIN AND DAY

			U.S.	CAN.
	8134-6	**THE MAN WHO WAS NOT HIMSELF** John Creasey	2.95	3.50
	8170-2	**THE MASTERPIECE AFFAIR** Kenneth Royce	2.95	3.50
	8133-8	**THIS MAN DID I KILL?** John Creasey as Kyle Hunt	2.95	3.50
	8161-3	**THE MINIATURES FRAME** Kenneth Royce	2.95	3.50
	8062-5	**OUTBREAK** Lionel Black	2.95	NCR
	8038-2	**SERGEANT VERITY AND THE IMPERIAL DIAMOND #1** Francis Selwyn	2.95	NCR
	8050-1	**SERGEANT VERITY AND THE SWELL MOB #2** Francis Selwyn	2.95	NCR
	8094-3	**THE SIN EATER** Elizabeth Walter	2.95	NCR
	8020-X	**TELL NO TALES** Gina Day	2.95	NE
	8141-9	**THE XYY MAN** Kenneth Royce	2.95	*